The Witches' Mark

The Witches' Mark

Donald Lightwood

Kelpies

Kelpies is an imprint of Floris Books

First published in Kelpies in 2006
Published in 2006 by Floris Books
Copyright © 2006 Donald Lightwood

The publisher acknowledges a Lottery grant
from the Scottish Arts Council towards the
publication of this series.

British Library CIP Data available

ISBN-10 0-86315-572-3
ISBN-13 978-086315-572-7

Produced in Poland by Polskabook

1

The witch stood on the small green that overlooked the harbour. She was alone, but everyone in the village was watching her. Women huddled in their shawls against the bitter wind. Tradesmen, idle for the moment from their work. The fishermen clustered by their boats that should have been at sea.

Somebody threw a stone. It landed at the witch's feet. Several more followed and one hit her on the shoulder.

Some of the crowd cheered. Others were fearful about annoying her. What if she put a curse on them? Arguments broke out. There were scuffles. Threats were shouted.

The witch, known as Old Pheemie, ignored the abuse. She had come to the harbour to see if what she had heard was true. That the wind had turned and the boats couldn't get out. Right enough, the wind was coming in from the sea, whipping up waves that crashed on the beach. It was true. The fish boxes piled around the harbour would stay empty.

A shout went up. "Where's the minister? He should be here."

"Him — he's a sweetie wife," cried one of the skippers.

"You're right there. The witch should be burnt at the stake."

"The nerve of the old baggage. Coming here."

"It's her fault."

The people of the small fishing community were sure they had right on their side. It was the law of the land.

Witches were evil and should be done away with. In the old days Pheemie's presence would not have been tolerated. But now, since King Charles II had been on the throne, the authorities had become slack. It was a disgrace.

The groups gathered together and moved towards Pheemie. But they soon reached a point beyond which no one was brave enough to go. It was as though there was a magical barrier surrounding the witch.

Now the crowd was openly confronting her there was silence. There were no more cries for her death. No one wanted to be identified and risk the witch's anger. And so the only sounds to be heard were the ill-favoured wind and the screeching seagulls.

Pheemie had experienced many such moments in her long life. She had survived because she understood that people are easily led and do foolish things. As an ugly old woman she had few weapons to fight the prejudice against her. They called her a witch, and so she let them believe it, since they were frightened of witches. But while it protected her, she knew it was dangerous. It was not uncommon for witches to be tortured and put to death. She had to keep her wits about her.

There was a silly giggling laugh, that turned into cries of pain. The crowd gasped in annoyance. It was Glaiket Jock, the village daftie, being punished for what he couldn't help. Pheemie felt sorry for the lad — like her, he was always being picked on.

She was determined to make them speak first. The rumour was that she had changed the direction of the wind so that the fishermen couldn't put out to sea. More evidence of their foolishness. How could they imagine she possessed the supernatural powers to perform such a feat? She was more used to them blaming her for a cow having a stillborn calf, or the hens not laying. This thing was madness. If she had that sort of power she could rule the world.

A murmur went up from the crowd. Someone had let loose a dog, a vicious looking bull mastiff. There was a tremor of excitement. They were going to have their revenge. The old hag would get her just desserts for doing the Devil's work.

The dog stood looking at Pheemie. The crowd urged it on and were rewarded with a growl, and then a snarl. The beast's fangs dripped with saliva, as though anticipating the taste of blood.

This was going to be good. The crowd approved whole-heartedly. They would be rid of the witch. No need for a trial, with do-gooders like the minister to speak for her. And with the dog to do their work, everyone would be innocent of her death. It was perfect. And a grand spectacle too.

The dog barked and went closer to Pheemie. It barked again and appeared to be ready to spring at her. Those watching could already picture fangs biting into flesh.

Pheemie remained still. If she was frightened, she did not show it. She regarded the dog calmly. The dog snarled, but her gaze did not falter. The crowd expected her to put up her arms to protect herself. She did not. Her only movement was to tilt her head a little to the side. It looked as if she was communicating with the animal — questioning it. After a tense moment, the dog's head also tilted to the side.

The old woman smiled, stooped a little, and put out her hand. The dog went to her and she fondled its ears, like a grannie petting her cat at the fireside. And then the vicious mastiff lay down at her feet, rested its snout on its forepaws and went to sleep.

Outrage flared up in the crowd. Denied the pleasure of seeing the witch torn to pieces, they screamed abuse at her. But as before, nobody dared cross the invisible barrier. They may have been furious, but they had just witnessed Pheemie's black art practised in front of their eyes. She had bewitched the dog. What else might she do?

Pheemie felt the warmth of the dog at her feet. It was a comfort. Never having had a friend, she had grown to enjoy the company of animals. They were trusting and never let you down. And because they seemed to sense the same in her, a special relationship had developed. She knew people called her way with animals black magic, but she didn't care. Everything she did was branded in the same way.

Two men pushed their way forward through the crowd. They were Bailie John Reekie, the magistrate, and the town officer, who was armed with a long pike.

"Be on your way, you're creating a disturbance," the Bailie told Pheemie. He was a strong, well-built man and a fisherman to trade. As magistrate, he took his duties seriously, but like now, did not find them easy.

"It's them. I'm just standing here."

"She put a spell on the dog," cried a voice.

"And the wind," added another. "You know fine we can't take the boats out, Bailie."

"There's no proof she's to blame," said the Bailie.

"She's a witch — that's proof enough."

There was a roar of approval.

"If we had a minister worth his salt, she'd have been put to the test and found guilty," came a shout.

The Bailie held up his hand to quieten them. "Witch trials are a thing of the past ..."

"No they're not. A witch was burnt in Dundee not long since."

"Aye — burn her!"

"The Church believes we should not rush to judgment," shouted the Bailie. "The civil authorities must respect their teaching in these matters."

"She's doing the Devil's work," responded Jamie Findlay, one of the skippers. "Try taking your own boat out John. See how far you get. *There's* your evidence."

"That would not stand in a court of law," said the Bailie.

"She's outside the law — like Old Nick himself."

The crowd roared agreement.

Fearful of where their anger might lead, the Bailie ordered the town officer to escort Pheemie out of the village. "I don't want any more trouble from you," he told her.

"It's these ignorant fishermen you need to worry about, not me," she replied.

"Hold your tongue," snapped the town officer, threatening her with his pike.

The dog growled. "Hush now," said Pheemie, patting its head. "I've to be on my way." As the man led her away many in the crowd spat and crossed their fingers to ward off evil.

Jamie Findlay went to the Bailie. "A fine magistrate you are," he said sarcastically. "Our bairns are going hungry because we can't fish and you do nothing."

"I can't change the wind, Jamie."

"No, but *she* can. If you won't get rid of her, we'll do it ourselves."

Though he was feeling anything but amused, the Bailie smiled. "Show me the fisherman brave enough to go near her. I should know. I'm one myself."

The appearance of the laird on his vessel was the last thing Ian Paterson wanted. It was the middle of the night and he had been asleep in his bunk.

"I've told you Sir Robert, there's nothing I can do," he told the man. "The wind's against us."

"Damn it, it shouldn't be!" shouted the laird. As one of the gentry, Sir Robert was used to getting his own way. When he didn't, he soon lost his fine manners and turned into a bully.

"I agree, sir. Never in all my seafaring days have I known a contrary wind to hold for so long. We can but wait for a south-westerly to blow up."

"I'm paying you well to get this cargo to Holland."

"I know sir," said the captain.

"There must be something you can do." The laird paced the small cabin like a caged animal.

"She's so laden, sir."

"You're saying the cargo is at fault?"

"It does not help, the holds being so full."

Sir Robert Abercrombie had bought up the bulk of the local grain harvest, intending to sell it abroad at a good profit. However the captain knew that there was not enough left for the townspeople and many were going hungry. And with the men unable to fish, the situation had become worse. Secretly he worried that people might take the law into their own hands and storm his vessel. They had to have food.

The laird shook his head. "There has got to be a reason."

The captain uncorked a bottle of spirits. "You'll take a dram, Sir Robert?" he said uncomfortably.

The laird eyed him. "You know something," he said suspiciously. "What is it? Speak out man."

"I think we are cursed," said the captain, lowering his voice. "We have lost our luck."

"What do you mean?"

"This boat. That's what the crew think."

The laird threw up his hand, dismissing the idea. "They're just a bunch of ignorant deckhands. They're as bad as the fishermen, full of superstitious nonsense."

"I know sir, but you have to admit, it is uncanny. Nobody has a natural explanation."

The laird took his glass, but he drank without enjoyment. Before long the whole damned town would know what he had on board. The boat had to be shifted. "And the other vessels — you think they are cursed as well?"

"That seems to be the way of it," said the captain. "All I can tell you is, a lone black crow was seen flying around the harbour, just before this began. The men tried to scare it away, but it perched on every boat before it disappeared."

"So what are you saying?"

"All the seamen believe it was the witch, Sir Robert," the captain told him.

"The crow?"

The captain nodded gravely. "It's well known that witches and the like take on the form of animals to do the Devil's work."

The laird glared at the captain, but he did not contradict him. Sir Robert was a well-educated man. As a student at St Andrews University in the 1660s he had often debated the supernatural origins of evil and how it could be overcome. He had seen witches tortured until they died. As agents of the Devil, it was regarded as a just fate. However he found it difficult to accept what the captain was suggesting. "Do you believe that?"

The man shrugged his shoulders. "I cannot think of a natural reason for what's happened."

Sir Robert scratched his head. "I've heard of her so-called spells. Crow or not, she may still be the one to blame."

"I agree," said the captain. "And if you'll forgive me, Sir Robert, there's likely to be trouble if we don't get out to sea. Folk know there's grain on board and ..."

"I know all that," the laird interrupted him. He'd got to take action — but what could he do? He felt trapped. If the witch was responsible, then it seemed most likely that she was the only person who could undo what she had done.

He hesitated at the thought. How could she be persuaded to do that?

2

A cock crowed. There was a pink glow in the east.
Dawn. The night was coming to an end and the wind
was still blowing in off the sea.

Pheemie pushed open the door of her hovel and
stepped out. She lived in the woods just outside the
fishing village and it suited her to be surrounded by
trees. Glancing round her garden of herbs and wild
flowers, she sniffed with pleasure. The birds were
already singing away.

The cock crowed again and Pheemie called good
morning to him. He was perched in a tree. His hens
were roosting down below in the bushes.

Pheemie's big black cat rubbed itself against her
legs. "It's going to be a wet day," she said, as the sky
began turning red. She cocked her head and listened.
With a snort, she set off through the trees. The cat
followed, treading delicately in her footsteps to avoid
getting wet in the dew.

She was heading to where a fifteen-year-old boy was
hiding in a coppice. Tall for his age, ginger-haired and
adventurous, he could feel the damp seeping into his
breeks. He fingered the few whiskers newly sprouted
on his chin and wished he was somewhere else. His
name was Murdo and he worked on Jamie Findlay's
boat. But like the rest of the crew, he had been sent
away yet again, even though the tide had been full.
Spying on the witch was a dare the fisherlads set each
other and it was Murdo's turn. Others had come back
with stories of seeing her flying and doing spells. He'd

only half believed them, but when he saw her coming straight towards him, he froze in terror.

"I know you're there," she called. "Who are you and what do you want?"

Murdo felt something by his leg. It was the cat. He jumped away from it in fear, showing himself to Pheemie.

She snorted. "Another brave laddie come to spy on the witch."

Murdo couldn't speak. He had never been so close to a witch before. She was peering at him and he imagined the horrible things she might do to him. Coming here was the most stupid thing he'd ever done. The cat rubbed against his legs and he let out a cry. Pheemie gave a wheezing laugh. "My cat likes you," she said. "He's called Snowball."

"But he's black," Murdo couldn't help responding, and then bit his tongue. Contradicting a witch was asking for trouble.

"So he is. All over."

It must be something to do with her magic, Murdo thought. He had heard that things were done backwards in witchcraft. He risked looking at Pheemie more closely. She seemed to be very old. Her face was deeply wrinkled and her lips looked sucked into her mouth. What he noticed most were her eyes, which were surprisingly bright and lively. He felt weak and foolish under her gaze.

"Have you nothing to say for yourself?" she asked him.

"How did you know I was here?"

Pheemie pointed up into the trees. "My friends, the birds. They chattered a warning as loud as the church bell. You'll need to do better than that if you want to creep up on folk."

"I'm sorry."

"Everybody wants to spy on the witch. Don't ask me why."

Murdo frowned. She must know. "You're different from other folk."

"I'm just an old woman. No different from your grannie."

"I don't have a grannie."

"You know fine what I mean," Pheemie said irritably. She was growing cold and should have sent him on his way.

And then Murdo got the shock of his life. Snowball jumped up into his arms. He almost lost his balance and had to cling on to the cat. Feeling the animal's wet fur against his face, he panicked. He was holding a witch's cat!

Pheemie chuckled at his discomfort. "You have a way with animals," she told him.

"No I haven't," he cried.

"Snowball's very fussy who he makes friends with."

The cat's purr was so loud in his ear, he could hardly hear what Pheemie was saying.

"Animals know who they can trust," she went on. "They're more clever than folk think." The cock crowed and it gave her an idea. "Come with me," she told him. Murdo tried to encourage the cat to jump down, so that he could run away. But it clung on to him, still purring happily. Pheemie called to him and he found himself following her.

She led him through the garden to her hovel. "Look under those bushes and see if the hens have laid any eggs," she said, taking Snowball from him. "I'm not so good at bending down these days."

Glad to be rid of the cat, he discovered the hens nesting and felt under them. While he was doing so, the cock flew down and stood at his side watching him. Murdo eyed the cock nervously.

"See, you do have a way with animals," said Pheemie. "He'd peck you to pieces if he didn't like you."

Murdo gave her four eggs and turned to hurry away.

"I'm going to cook these for breakfast," she told him. "You can have some if you want, for helping me."

"I'd best be on my way."

"Are you not hungry?"

He'd had to be up at four o'clock to catch the tide and he was starving. But the thought of eating the witch's food scared him. He shook his head.

"There's nothing to be frightened of," she said. "I'll not poison you."

The cock crowed.

"See, *he* wants you to stay," she went on.

They were lovely looking eggs ... And his belly was aching for food. He took a breath and nodded.

Pheemie's hovel was poorly furnished. A bed, a crude table, two stools, a sea chest, and an old range, on which she cooked the eggs. Snowball sat on the chest and watched the two eat. Murdo had rarely had such a tasty meal. But much as he'd enjoyed it, he was still fearful. Like everybody in Scotland in the seventeenth century, he had been brought up to believe in the evil of witch-craft. Misbehaving children were always being told the witch would get them if they didn't mend their ways. And yet here he was, eating a witch's food. "Save some for the cat," Pheemie told him. "He likes a bit of egg."

Murdo put his platter on the floor and Snowball jumped down and licked it clean.

"That was good," he said. "Thank you."

She warmed her hands at the fire glowing in the range. "So, you don't have a grannie."

"I don't have nobody."

"Where do you live?"

"In the fishermen's bothy."

She grunted. "Then I'm sorry for you."

He frowned at her reply. "Why's that?"

"If there is a more ignorant and superstitious bunch of loons on God's earth, I've yet to hear of them," she told him.

"I work on the boats. I have to stay there."

"You'll be done for if they hear you've been here with me."

He nodded miserably. "Aye, it's likely."

She regarded him for a moment. "Yet you stayed?"

"I was hungry."

"Most folk would rather starve to death than eat with a witch."

He didn't know what to say and looked at the cat. It immediately jumped up onto his lap.

Pheemie smiled. "For what it's worth son, I'll tell you again. I'm not a witch. You're in no danger from me — no matter what they say in the village. I know you'll find it hard to believe, but it's the truth. For my sins I've got a hump on my back and an ugly face. So I'm called a witch."

"Folk say you've done things," said Murdo.

She nodded. "Aye. It's useful to have somebody to blame when things go wrong. Like the turnabout in the wind. Look at me — d'you think I could do that?"

He couldn't meet her gaze and squirmed uncomfortably.

"They say you do magic spells."

"And what do *you* say?"

Murdo couldn't answer. Without thinking he stroked the cat. She seemed all right. But that could be part of her magic. And she seemed kind — she'd given him breakfast. But it was hard to forget his upbringing.

Pheemie sighed. "I used to pray that one day I'd meet somebody who was not suspicious of me. It never happened, and it never will. They'll go on making up stories about me till the day I die. My only prayer now is that I'll end my days in my bed, and not on a bonfire."

What she said shocked him. It was a terrible thought. "They wouldn't do that," he protested.

"Yes they would," she said.

He shook his head. "It used to happen. Not now."

"It still happens," she told him.

Murdo remembered the mood of the crowd at the harbour, when they were shouting at Pheemie. He shivered. The cat stopped purring and looked up at him. He tried not to think of flames licking round the old woman who had been kind to him. "It's wrong," he said.

Pheemie was quiet for a few moments. Then she spoke again. "What is your name?" she asked. He told her and she nodded her head. "Whatever happens, always be true to yourself, Murdo."

The cat suddenly jumped off his lap and leapt onto the sill of the small window. The angry red sky outside was reflected in its eyes.

Pheemie spoke to the cat. "I know, I heard." She got up, pulling her shawl about her. "I have to go out," she told Murdo. "Stay here. You'll be safe." She went out and shut the door.

Still surprised, he sat looking at the door and then went to the window. The cat was staring out. They saw Pheemie standing in the garden, looking towards the track just beyond it. The cat made a growling noise.

"What is it?" said Murdo, as though expecting an answer from the animal. He could see nothing, but soon heard the creaking of a farm cart. Then he saw it, being led by one man, with two others on either side. They were carrying swords.

One of the men saw Pheemie and cried out. The cart stopped. The two men with swords glanced at each other. Murdo could see they were frightened.

"You've got to come with us," they shouted at Pheemie.

"Who says?" she retorted.

"The laird. He's wanting to see you."

"I'm not wanting to see him."

"You're to come. Get in the cart."

Pheemie nodded her head slowly. "I'll remember you two," she told them.

"That's enough from you," said the first man, his fear showing through. "Get round the back of her, Rab."

They circled Pheemie, threatening her with their swords. "In the cart with you ..."

They herded her like a beast. "My word, you're brave," said Pheemie, sitting down in the cart. "Three grown men to get an old woman. I doubt you're dab hands at robbing sweeties off the bairns."

Murdo watched the cart trundle away. Snowball scratched at the door and he let the cat out.

It started to rain.

Pheemie whispered to the mouse and it climbed onto her hand. She lifted it up and it nuzzled her cheek. She was sitting on a heap of straw in one of the laird's stables. The horses had been taken away so that she couldn't bewitch them.

Back on the floor, the mouse twitched its whiskers and scampered away. Pheemie smiled. Thank God for animals, they were her only friends. Even as a lass people had kept clear of her. Other girls had been told how pretty they were. But she had grown up hearing only that the good Lord had seen fit to punish her by making her ugly. Not that her mother had complained. She had been a beggar and used her deformed daughter to help her open up people's purses. It had taught Pheemie that the worst curse of all was to be different.

The rain drummed on the roof. She thought about the fisherlad Murdo. He'd called her witch like all the rest, but she had enjoyed talking to him. It was sad that youngsters like him should grow up amongst such prejudice. He was the only person she had ever met who had shown any concern for her.

The stable door opened and the laird strode in. He was carrying a riding crop. He stood closer to Pheemie than anyone else had dared. "I am Sir Robert Abercrombie, laird of these parts. You are to answer my questions."

"Why?" said Pheemie.

"Because I say so," said Sir Robert. "You were seen at the harbour. Why were you there?"

"A body has to be somewhere or other."

"What was your purpose there?"

She shrugged her shoulders and sniffed.

He cracked his riding crop on his boot. "There was a barque tied up there — the *Fife Lassie,*" he told her. "You were seen looking at it."

"Then I must have been."

"Why?"

Pheemie scratched her nose. "I remember now. They were loading it with grain."

"And you were watching them. Why?"

"I'd never seen so much," she replied. "It looked like the whole harvest. I was thinking you'd have to be stinking rich to have all that."

"That cargo happens to belong to me," he said.

"So I heard."

"Who told you?" he demanded.

"Everybody knows."

He went on angrily. "I have reason to believe you stopped that vessel sailing. Why did you do that? Is somebody paying you?"

Pheemie shook her head. "From what I heard, nobody wants it to sail. Except you and me."

He stared at her in surprise. *"You?"*

"Aye."

"... I don't understand."

"It's their own fault," she said.

He was perplexed. "Who are you talking about?"

She looked at him as if he was simple-minded. "The folk in this town. They brought it on themselves."

"Stop talking in riddles," he ordered. "Brought *what* on themselves?"

"Not having any food," she responded. "Seeing your boat sail away might wake them up."

The laird looked at her suspiciously. "To what?"

"That they need to do something about you, Sir Robert, if they don't want to starve."

He raised his riding crop threateningly. "Watch your mouth, you old crone."

"And you'd best watch your temper, or you'll get nothing out of me." She fixed him with her eyes and he backed off.

He changed his tone. "You are a poor woman. I can give you money. All I ask is that you do what you have to do to make that boat sail."

"You need a good wind to do that," said Pheemie.

"I know that. I want you to make one.

"Is that why you've brought me here? You think I can do that?"

He controlled himself with difficulty. "You have unearthly powers."

She sucked at her toothless gums, considering him. "And if I do it, you'll let me go?"

"You have my word," he told her.

She chuckled. "I've heard tell that's worth no more than thistledown on the wind."

"Damn it, I promise," he said through his teeth.

She stood up. "I can't do it here. I'm cold and wet."

The laird hesitated. Much as he wanted to free the *Fife Lassie,* he was nervous about becoming involved in witchcraft. Tampering with the supernatural was dangerous. "What do you have to do?" he asked, all the bluster gone out of his voice.

"You tell me I'm a witch," she said. "I'll do what witches have to do."

"Do I have your word that it will not taint the castle?"

"What?"

"The spell, or whatever you call it." He could hardly bring himself to utter the word.

She gave him her toothless grin. "Your castle will be safe from anything I do."

He regarded her doubtfully. But he knew he had no choice now that he was committed. He led her out.

They crossed the courtyard to the back entrance of the castle. Stairs descended under the building to the heavily vaulted chambers that housed the kitchens and the servants' quarters.

There were screams when the cook and two kitchen lassies saw Pheemie. They pulled their aprons over their heads and ran out as fast as they could.

Pheemie paid no attention to them and placed herself in front of the large fireplace, with its spits and trivets. Sir Robert Abercrombie kept his distance, watching her every move. She waved him away and he left the room gladly, not wanting to be party to her weird goings-on.

Pheemie's first act was to move closer to the fire and warm her legs. Her damp clothes steamed. From where she stood she could see through a window, high up in the wall. The rain had almost stopped and the sky was getting lighter.

The kitchen had a good smell. There was food everywhere in different stages of preparation. Pheemie chuckled to herself. Before she thought any more about what she might do, she would have something to eat.

The laird paced back and forth in his study. He had to be careful. Whichever way he looked at it, he was an accomplice to witchcraft. It was a subject about which people lost all sense of reason. His rank and position normally protected him. But it was still a risk. As soon as he had got what he wanted, he would get rid of her. Once she was dead he would be safe.

In the kitchen Pheemie finished a bowl of broth and looked out of the window. She smiled at what she saw. She stood up, squinting to make sure. The top branches of the laird's trees were starting to sway. She sat down again and crossed her fingers for good luck. To fill in the time, she looked round the kitchen and wondered what she would steal.

The clatter of a two wheeled gig drew Sir Robert to the front entrance of the castle. He brushed aside a servant and threw open the door himself. Bailie Reekie and the town officer got down and approached him.

"What do you want?" Sir Robert demanded.

"Old Pheemie," said the Bailie.

"What the devil are you talking about?"

"You've got her here and I order you to release her into our custody," the Bailie told him.

"*You* order *me?*" bellowed the laird.

"Aye, I do, Sir Robert."

"I think I should remind you who I am," said Sir Robert. "I am a Baronet of the Realm and your feudal superior. *I* give the orders here."

"I'm speaking as the duly elected magistrate."

"Be on your way," said the laird. "She's not here."

"I don't believe you."

"You doubt my word?"

"I have a witness who saw your men take the old woman away," the Bailie replied. He nodded to the town officer, who went to the gig and revealed Murdo. "This lad saw them."

The laird looked at Murdo with contempt. "He's just a boy," he said.

"Maybe. But he has eyes in his head."

The laird's outrage built up alarmingly, the worse for being tinged with fear. All he could do was bluster his way out of the situation. "Get off my property," he shouted.

The town officer let out a sudden cry. A sharp breeze had blown off his tricorn hat and sent it spinning over the cobbles. He chased after it, embarrassed at the indignity to his office.

Standing his ground in front of the laird, the Bailie was astonished at Sir Robert's reaction. For a moment it looked as if he had been turned to stone. His shouting was silenced and his eyes popped. Then his mouth fell open.

"The wind," he muttered. "The wind's changed ..."

He turned on his heel and ran towards the stables. "My horse, saddle my horse. My horse, dammit ... hurry, hurry."

A commotion broke out in the castle. Servants were running about and shouting. They appeared at the door armed with brooms and sticks, prodding Pheemie to get her outside.

"Leave her be," the Bailie called to them. "She's coming along with us."

"What brings you here, Bailie?" said the old woman.

"This young man was worried for your safety," he replied. Pheemie looked at Murdo. "That was kind of you, son," she told him.

"Did he hurt you?" Murdo asked.

She shook her head. "No, I was lucky."

The Bailie addressed Murdo. "How did you come to see what happened? You haven't told me that."

Realizing that Murdo didn't know what to say, Pheemie answered for him. "He comes to collect my eggs. I can't bend down no more and he's a help to me."

A strong wind was blowing as the four rode back in the gig. Pheemie held on to a bag of food she'd taken from the laird's kitchen. Not for the first time she thanked her mother, who had taught her many things about the countryside. A red sky in the morning was the shepherd's warning. Most folk knew that. But she wondered how many knew one of her other sayings. *'The harder the rain, the harder the wind that follows.'*

The town officer was holding his hat on with one hand and clutching the reins with the other. He shouted to the Bailie. "The laird's boat should be making sail by now."

The Bailie gave a contented smile. His years as a seaman on the east coast of Fife had taught him what wind you needed to get out of the harbour. "I very much doubt it," he said. "It's a grand wind — but it's blowing in the wrong direction."

3

Once more the laird confronted the captain in his cabin.

"Don't you blame me!" roared the captain. "This damn wind's blowing the wrong way round."

Sir Robert glared back at him. "You're drunk, man," he responded angrily.

"So would you be, if you'd been stuck here on this God forsaken vessel. I tell you it is cursed. This wind was the last straw for the crew. They've abandoned ship. You'll not find a seaman who will step on board."

"This is mutiny!" cried the laird. "I'll have every last one of them hanged."

The captain took a swig from his glass and gave him a drunken grin. "Folk are more likely to hang you."

"Watch your tongue."

"The whole town knows your game by now. And I would remind you, Sir Robert, with no crew, there's nobody to protect your cargo. You'd do well to think on that."

A shiver of fear ran up the laird's back. He was trapped in an impossible position. Anger seethed inside him. The grain could not be left unguarded.

"Seemingly Old Pheemie fooled you," sneered the captain.

"She has cast her last spell," snapped Sir Robert. "You may be sure of that."

"If you mean what I think you mean, take care."

"I do not need advice from you."

The captain looked at him insolently. "You could say she has done the community a favour — stopping you shipping out the grain. Folk might not be so anxious to see her harmed now."

The laird clenched his teeth. The man was probably right. He must think of some other way of revenging himself against the witch. But he would. By God he would. Nobody humiliated him. Least of all an ugly old baggage with no teeth.

"Unload the grain," he ordered the captain.

"How? I've got no crew."

"I'll send men, carts. I'll sell it locally."

The captain staggered to his feet. "Very wise, Sir Robert, if I may say so."

"Sober yourself up, you drunken sot," replied the laird, struggling to open the cabin door against the wind.

The captain lunged after him. "Sir Robert, there is the question of the vessel's hire. I know we didn't get to Holland, but ..."

Sir Robert pushed the man away and sent him sprawling.

The next market day was more like a fair. There was plenty of grain and meal on sale, and it was being said that the herring had started to run again. The old men claimed it was due to the same on-shore wind that had kept the *Fife Lassie* storm bound. Whatever the reason, the fisher families were full of good cheer in the market square.

The appearance of Old Pheemie at the market caused consternation. There was a rumour that she was responsible for the laird's boat not sailing. If it was true, she had saved them from starvation. A few people shouted abuse at her, but they were quickly silenced. Didn't they realize they were in the witch's debt?

The crowd parted respectfully as she went round the stalls. It was as though you could hear the thought uppermost in people's mind: "How had she done it?" She had changed the wind yet again — this time for the good of all. And the fact that she had foiled the laird's plans added spice. He was a detested landlord and it served him right.

Everyone watched as Pheemie bought some oats.

"How much?" she asked, as the stall keeper weighed up a small sack for her.

"Don't make her pay," someone called out.

"Give them to her," cried another, to general agreement.

The stall keeper responded. "There's no charge, Pheemie."

She looked round the circle of curious faces. "Why not?" she said.

The man seemed shy. "I couldn't ask you to pay."

"Is everybody getting their oats free?" she asked.

There was a burst of laughter from the crowd. "We didn't get our own back on the laird," someone called out to her.

"I didn't do nothing," she told them.

They didn't believe her.

"You did so. Little he cares if we go hungry ..."

"... He's just out for himself, him."

A chorus of agreement rang out.

Pheemie stood facing them, shaking her head. "I'm sick of telling you, I can't do these things. And you can take it from me, if I had the skills of witchcraft, I wouldn't stay here. I'd do a spell and fly away and find some sensible folk who'd give me peace."

"It *was* you. Nobody else could have changed the wind."

"The weather looks after itself," she told them. "As the fishermen know fine. Leastways they would, if they weren't so simple minded."

There was laughter at this, but Pheemie knew they were not convinced. It was as though they wanted a witch, whatever she said. A nervous voice spoke up from the crowd. "Is it true it's the Devil tells you what to do, Pheemie?"

Shocked protests made clear this was going too far — mentioning the evil one by name. As if they hadn't had enough bad luck.

Pheemie lost her temper. "Aye!" she cried out. "Old Nick and me get drunk together, every Saturday night!" She turned her back on them and started to drag her sack away.

"Let me help you with that," said a boy, stepping out of the crowd. It was Murdo. He heaved the sack onto his back and set off with the old woman.

The morning was like the answer to a fisherman's prayer. Nobody dared say it, but all was set fair for a good day's fishing. The wind was favourable and the tide running just as it should. Perfect.

Murdo and his friend Alex tumbled out of their beds, both keen to set sail. They pulled on their clothes and Alex kicked open the door of the bothy. He was a few months younger than Murdo, but equally strong and always determined not to let his friend get the better of him.

"It's a fine day."

Murdo was breaking some bread for them to chew on their way. "Hurry, maybe we can be first out."

As the boys hurried along they glanced about warily. It was bad luck to see a woman on the way to the fishing. Seeing the minister was even worse. Meeting him

meant the fisherman had to return home, take off his
hat and sit down. If he was unlucky enough to see the
minister a second time, he had no choice but to aban-
don his day's fishing.

Both of them crewed on Jamie Findlay's boat. When
they arrived, the skipper was standing on the quay
talking to Bailie John Reekie. They were looking out
to sea.

"It's uncanny, John," said Jamie.

"Aye. I've never seen the herring in so close before.
Though I mind my father telling me he'd seen it as a
young man."

They watched a large swarm of gulls screaming over
the sea, no more than half a mile out. A sure sign that
a shoal lay underneath.

"How do you account for it?" asked Jamie. "We go
from having nothing, to this."

John Reekie shook his head. "All I can think is the
good Lord has looked kindly upon us."

"I would like to think that was the reason."

"I can think of no other."

Jamie spat on the quay and rubbed the spittle with
his boot. "There's been queer ongoings lately."

"Away with you, man," said John. "Be thankful.
Think of your wife and bairns. They'll be glad of a good
catch, even if you're not."

"Not if it's tainted with sorcery, they'll not."

"What makes you think that?"

"You know fine," retorted Jamie.

"If you're meaning the business with Old Pheemie,
I think you're wide of the mark," John told him.
"We've been fishing our whole lives. If there's one
thing we know about fish, it is that they're fickle
creatures. They come and go for no reason whatsoever."

Jamie grunted, unconvinced. A flock of gannets had joined the gulls and were diving for the fish, which flashed silver in their beaks.

"We'll not have far to go for a good catch today," said Murdo, grinning at the two men.

"I doubt we'll ever have it easier," said John.

Jamie spoke to Murdo as he prepared to climb into his boat. "I'm not wanting you on board," he told him.

"Why not?" asked Murdo in surprise.

"I don't, that's all."

Murdo stepped back onto the quay with a look at John Reekie.

"What's got into you, Jamie?" said John.

"He's too familiar with yon old witch woman. He could bring bad luck."

"No, I won't!" Murdo protested.

Jamie was unyielding. "How do you know? An animal doesn't know it brings bad luck on board. But it does."

"What will I do?" said Murdo, almost in tears.

John Reekie spoke to him. "You wait here. We'll need extra help to unload today's catch."

None of the fishermen preparing their boats were given to showing their feelings. But as the crew loaded their nets, there was an air of anticipation that cracked dour faces into smiles. Five or six sailed in each boat and they took pride in their rowing and shooting their nets cleanly. They had a share in the catch and worked hard for the good of each other.

At the moment the small fleet was due to cast off, there came sudden cries of panic from the far end of the harbour. Men stood up in their boats to discover what was going on. When they saw what was happening, they too joined in the shouting and commotion. Soon the fleet was in uproar.

To anyone from outside the fishing community the cause of the disturbance would have seemed ridiculous. The figure of Glaiket Jock, the town daftie, had appeared on the harbour, leading a pig on a length of rope. Only the presence of the Devil himself would have caused greater consternation amongst the fishermen. To them the pig was the most dreaded of animals.

"Cold iron! Cold iron!" The cry rose up as the men rushed to touch the nearest iron object. Only by doing that could the pig's curse be avoided. Evil spirits poured forth from the hole in the pig's trotter, making it the most malevolent of God's creatures.

Nobody dared go near Glaiket Jock for fear of the animal. And the more they shouted at him, the more Jock became pleased with himself. His daft grin widened and he laughed out loud at the spectacle of these grown men cowering from him. He had power over them. Each one, at some time or another, had clouted him, or made fun of him. But now he could torment them.

It was simple. All he had to do was lead the pig a few steps forward, and the men fell over each other to get away from him. In his joy, he hugged the pig and kissed it on the snout. There were yells of outrage. Jock stuck out his tongue and danced a wee jig on the cobbles. Never before had he experienced the thrill that he now felt. He had his tormentors at his mercy.

John Reekie was as superstitious as the other fishermen and he had to force himself to take action. As the town Bailie it was his duty to do something. He stood on a fish box and shouted to the daftie.

"Jock, you know me. John Reekie, the Bailie. Take that animal away from here. Do you hear me? I'm ordering you. Take it away."

"Nah."

"If you don't, I'll have you put in the jail."

Jock twisted round and showed his bottom to the Bailie.

John didn't know what to do. But then he had an idea. "Is it money you're wanting, Jock?"

"Aye," said Jock, putting out his hand.

"Do you want a lot of money?"

"Aye."

"Then you'll need more than one hand for that," said John, coaxing the dim-witted lad. "You'll need *two* hands for a lot of money."

Jock immediately put out his other hand as well, letting go of the pig's rope.

The men bellowed with one voice and the terrified animal ran away. Realizing he'd been tricked, Jock gave a cry and ran after it. Nobody chased him. Much as they wanted to vent their anger on him, they knew the damage had been done. They could not go fishing. All sailing would have to be suspended until an ebb and flow of the tide had washed away the curse.

Grumbling, the crews unloaded the nets from their boats. The herring shoal now seemed even closer in, underlining their frustration. A day of easy fishing had been lost.

Jamie Findlay gave Murdo a vile look. "I knew there would be bad luck," he growled at John Reekie, who had no reply.

"I've been put off Jamie Findlay's boat," Murdo told Pheemie. She was sitting on a log outside her hovel, stroking Snowball.

"Listen to them," she said, nodding up at a clutch of blackbirds. "They're jealous of the cat."

Murdo wasn't in the mood to concern himself with birds. "I said ..."

"Aye, I heard." She didn't seem bothered. "So that's why you're here."

"I doubt I'll be able to get on another boat."

"It's no loss."

He looked at her in surprise. "What do you mean?"

"You're a bright lad. You don't want to waste your life with those daft loons."

"I've got to work."

"Not with them."

Didn't she understand? He had no choice in the matter. He'd been hoping for some sympathy and her response was disappointing. "There's no other boats," he said, irritation in his voice.

"They're more superstitious than their womenfolk," she said, rubbing the cat's ear.

"I know that," said Murdo. "But they know how to catch fish. They need good luck to do that. Every fisherman does. You can't blame them for trying to bring it about."

"Do you believe in good luck?" she asked.

"Of course."

"And bad luck?"

"Aye."

She grunted. "Like having a woman on a boat brings bad luck?"

"It does."

"How do you know?"

He shrugged his shoulders. "Everybody knows."

"How do they know?" Pheemie persisted.

"... Because they *do*," he replied, his irritation growing.

"Like they know I'm a witch," she said.

"I don't know how it happens," he retorted. It was as though she was blaming him for what people believed.

Pheemie took out a small clay pipe and started to fill it with tobacco. Watching her, Murdo couldn't help wondering how she kept it in her mouth with no teeth. "It's not your fault," she said.

"There are things you don't ask about."

"I know that well enough," Pheemie went on. "My mother was full of it. What you had to do to bring good luck. I asked her once how she came to have the bad luck to have an ugly daughter like me. She laughed, and kissed me, and told me it was good luck I was ugly. I made people feel sorry for her and they gave her money."

Murdo sighed. He'd never dared question what the fishermen believed and simply copied their behaviour, whether it was a superstition, or shooting the nets. Both were equally important to the crew. But after the episode with the pig, it had seemed odd to him that farmers were not frightened of the animal. Nobody would keep pigs if they were. It didn't make sense. "Why are pigs bad luck?" he asked Pheemie.

"They aren't, to sensible folk."

"But they are, to fishermen."

"I know."

"They wouldn't go out this morning because Glaiket Jock brought a pig to the harbour."

"That proves what I'm saying," she told him.

"Do you think it would have been safe for the boats to go out?" he asked.

"Aye, I do."

"But how do you know you're right?"

She went inside to light her pipe from the fire. When it was going, she stood in the doorway and answered his question.

"I'll tell you," she said. "There was a time, years ago, when I tried to become a real witch. I was called

one, so I thought to myself, I might as well be one.
I never went to the kirk, so it was easy to turn my
back on God. But it was necessary to get in touch
with the Devil, and that was not so easy. You have
to make what they call a pact with him. Somehow I
had to meet him. I tried everything I'd heard about
from my mother and other superstitious old bod-
ies. Swearing, blaspheming, dancing at midnight,
repeating the Lord's Prayer backwards. And all the
rest. They said the Devil would come disguised as an
animal. He didn't." She chuckled. "When I think of
the poor beasts I surprised — asking if they were Old
Nick." She shook her head. "Don't ask me how, but all
superstitions are invented. It helps folk to think they
control things."

Murdo said nothing and watched Pheemie smoking
her pipe. She didn't keep it in her mouth, like the old
men, but held it with her hand and sucked at it now
and again. He noticed that Snowball did not like the
smell of the tobacco smoke and stalked off with his tail
in the air.

"So Glaiket Jock did his stuff," said Pheemie.

Murdo looked at her. "What do you mean?"

"I gave him a bawbee to take the pig to the boats."

"*You* did?"

"Aye."

"But you knew what would happen if he did," he said
in a shocked voice. "They lost a day's fishing."

"Serve them right."

"We need the fish. That wasn't fair."

She spat on the ground. "They're not fair to me. Nobody
is. Let them have a taste of their own medicine."

Murdo was appalled at what she had done. "But
don't you see, it will only make things worse for you, if
they find out you were responsible."

"I'm not fussed," she said. "They'll be feared I'll put another spell on them."

He stood up angrily. "You can't," he said. "You're not a witch."

Pheemie regarded him in silence, her pipe forgotten and the ghost of a smile twitching her wrinkled old mouth. "You and me know that," she said. "But they don't."

4

No fisherfolk went out into the dangers of the night. When dusk fell they shut themselves in and the village was as silent as a graveyard.

And so two moonlit figures went unobserved as they crept through the wooded glen behind the village. They were following the course of the burn and going towards the castle. Their unusual route had been dictated by Sir Robert's insistence on secrecy.

Tam, the laird's man, halted. The stranger behind him also stopped. A cloud had covered the moon and it had suddenly become pitch dark. The only sound came from their breathing. When the moon came back, the stranger clutched Tam's arm.

A shadowy form was moving on the other side of the burn. The stranger reached for his pistol, but Tam restrained him.

"Best wait till we get closer," he whispered. "Follow me."

They edged their way to the bank and hid behind a gorse bush. It went dark again and they lost sight of the ghostly figure. When the moon reappeared, they saw the person bent low, apparently scouring the ground.

"What's he doing?" hissed Tam.

An owl hooted.

The figure rose and looked up into the branches of a tree. The two men heard the faint sound of a voice.

"God save us," said the stranger. "He's talking to the owl."

Tam froze. "It's not a man. It's Old Pheemie, the witch."

"A witch?" There was a tremor of fear in the stranger's voice.

The owl hooted and they heard Pheemie chuckle. And then, amazingly, the owl flew down and perched on a lower branch next to the old woman.

The stranger drew in his breath sharply. "It's likely she's consorting with the Devil himself," he said.

Tam gulped. "You mean, the owl ...?

"It's what they do. It's how he appears to them — in the guise of an animal."

"God sakes," said Tam, trying to bite on his chattering teeth. "What will we do if she sees us?"

"Keep still," ordered the stranger. He watched her intently as she stooped down again.

"She's picking something," said Tam.

"It'll be for a spell. He's telling her what she needs. She's about the Devil's work, as sure as can be."

Nervously Tam eased his crouched body and a twig snapped under his foot. It sounded shockingly loud.

Pheemie looked up and peered across the burn. Tam and the stranger stopped breathing. It seemed she was staring straight at them. A cloud covered the moon. When the moonlight returned, Pheemie had disappeared.

She was already well on her way home with the mushrooms she had been collecting for her breakfast.

"Drink this," said the laird gruffly, giving the stranger a glass of brandy. Moir's pallid face was damp with sweat. "I ordered you never to come here," Sir Robert told him.

Moir paid no heed and gulped the brandy. Sir Robert paced the room, hoping none of the servants had seen who Tam had brought in out of the dark.

"Were you seen?" asked Sir Robert anxiously.

"That's of no account — it's what *we* saw!" cried Moir. "May God protect me from such a sight again."

He told Sir Robert how he and Tam had witnessed Pheemie's witchcraft.

The laird regarded him carefully. "Are you absolutely sure?" he asked.

"Of course I'm sure. I saw her with my own eyes."

"I mean — that she was doing the Devil's work."

Moir banged his glass down on the table. "I may not be a minister, but I know their ways as well as the next man."

"If you had kept our agreement, you would *not* have seen it," said Sir Robert impatiently.

"I had no choice but to come. We have important business to discuss."

"Get on with it then," said Sir Robert, showing his irritation.

Moir drew himself up in his seat. "Before I do, I would remind you that you are not talking to one of your servants. I am your partner in this business. You would do well to remember what I know about you, sir."

"Are you threatening me?" blustered Sir Robert.

"No sir. Simply reminding you."

There was a silence before Sir Robert's reply. He was aware that it would not be wise to offend the man, common though he was. "Very well," he said.

"In short, Sir Robert, you are failing in your side of our bargain," Moir told him. "Far too often the goods are not being brought ashore. That is your responsibility. For several nights now, my men have been left with nothing to put in their carts."

The laird's face coloured. "Manning the boats has been difficult of late."

"I had your assurance it would not be."

Sir Robert glared at him. The man's impertinence was breathtaking. How dare he address him in such a manner. "I have told you."

"I need to know what you are doing about it," said Moir. "I am losing money. I cannot sell fresh air. Folk want their brandy and tobacco. It's up to you to get us back on an even keel."

"It will be done. There has been a shortage of seamen."

"Why?" demanded Moir brusquely.

"They have become wary of going to sea."

"Meaning?"

"Just that," snapped Sir Robert.

Moir gave a thin smile. In spite of his partnership with Sir Robert, it gave him a malicious pleasure to see the man squirm. This highborn nobleman was not above playing the role of smuggler when it suited him. There appeared to be nothing he wouldn't do for money. But he still had the nerve to behave as if these illegal dealings were beneath him.

"So, I have your word you will make amends and our trade will resume in the near future?" said Moir.

His insolence pricked Sir Robert yet again. One day he would make Moir learn to respect his betters.

"I will send a message in the usual manner," he told him.

Moir nodded. "Sooner, rather than later, sir, I would hope. Now, there is something else we must discuss. The question of the witch. It concerns me. I smell danger."

"Do you indeed?"

"Yes sir, I do."

It was the laird's turn to smile. "I can't say I'm surprised. Superstition is rife among the lower classes."

"And with good reason," said Moir, noting the insult, but ignoring it. "There is well documented evidence of their evil doings."

Sir Robert snorted. "Witch trials serve one purpose only. To get rid of the accused woman. But do not delude yourself there is ever any real proof of their guilt."

"I am talking about what people know and see," said Moir. "Be it the Devil's will, or not, witchcraft upsets normal life. It can destroy communities."

Sir Robert realized the hardened trader had revealed a chink in his armour. "So, you fear her powers?"

"As any sane man would." Moir picked up his glass and examined the remaining dregs of brandy. "There is a story being told along the coast of a vessel you chartered being cursed."

"Idle gossip."

"And the contrary winds ...?" Moir raised an eyebrow. "You surely don't need reminding our goods come by sea from Holland?"

"I do not," said Sir Robert crisply. "As it happens, I already have a plan afoot to remove the menace that seems to worry you so much."

Moir gave a crooked smile. "So you admit, she does pose a danger?"

"I admit nothing, sir," retorted Sir Robert. "As far as I am concerned, we have concluded our business."

"Very well." Moir rose and moved to the door. "The success of our venture lies in your hands."

Murdo swung his axe and split another log. He would much rather have been out fishing with Alex, than chopping wood for Pheemie. He had come to her hovel to avoid the humiliation of being left on the harbour. His anger at Jamie Findlay gave him extra strength and he threw himself into his work. Each swing of his axe was a protest at Jamie's stupidity.

Pheemie was frying mushrooms and creating a delicious smell. She was humming a song she remembered her mother singing. Snowball was watching her, sensing that something was different. Pheemie smiled — both at the cat and at herself. Something *was* different. It was a feeling the old woman had thought she would never experience. She was happy.

Maybe she should have felt guilty that this had come about because of Murdo's misfortune. She was sorry for the lad, but his losing his job had brought them together and it seemed she had found a friend. Though she wondered if she should even think such a thought. She had spent her whole life as an outcast. Was it possible there was somebody who accepted her as a normal human being?

She put her head outside the door and called to Murdo. "Come and get something to eat, lad."

When he'd eaten his fill, Murdo left a few mushrooms and put his platter down for the cat. Snowball sniffed them and walked out.

"You finish them off yourself," said Pheemie. "Cats are fussy creatures."

"How do you know which mushrooms you can eat?" he asked.

"My mother learned me."

"My mother died when I was born," he said.

"That's an awful shame. What about your father?"

"I don't know who he was."

"Were they not married?" she asked and he shook his head. "It was the same with me. Born out of wedlock. They say it's a sin, as though it's your fault."

He shrugged. "You can't do nothing about it."

"No, you can't. So who looked after you?"

"My auntie. She called me her burden. I ran away as soon as I was old enough."

"And I doubt they bothered to look for you?" said Pheemie.

"No."

She regarded him. "Well you've grown up to be a strong young man."

"It's hard work on the boats," he said. "You need to be strong." He gave an exasperated sigh. "I'll have to go away to find work. Along the coast, to Pittenweem or Anstruther."

"You don't need to go for a wee while, surely," she said, trying not to sound anxious.

"I've got to get a job. And I'll have to get out of the bothy."

"You can stay here," she told him. "You could help me with the garden, and the hens and that."

He looked at her and almost laughed out loud. Living with a witch! It was the most astonishing thing he'd ever heard. Even though he didn't now believe she was a real witch — it's what people would think. But then he realized it didn't matter what they thought. He'd lost his job and didn't have to worry about folk in the village. He could imagine what Jamie Findlay would say. And it was that thought made him accept Pheemie's offer.

"I don't know nothing about growing stuff in gardens," he told her.

"You like eating it," she said. "That's a good start, you'll learn soon enough. When my mother was learning me about mushrooms and herbs, she said at first everything looks the same. That's because you're only *looking,* and not *seeing.* Like fishermen know the sea. To me it's just water — not to them. They can read it like a book."

He nodded. Though he hated the man, Jamie Findlay's understanding of the sea was uncanny.

"What you have to remember about plants, is that there's something special about each and every one of them. *That's* what you have to see. When you can do that, you learn to know them and respect them." She looked at him and chuckled. "Would you believe the dandelion is one of the cleverest plants you'll ever come across? That's why they're everywhere. Where folk and animals walk, they only grow wee, so they don't get crushed. But in the open and along the hedgerows, they grow tall. Is that not clever?"

"Aye, it is," he said.

"And they make good wine," she added with another chuckle.

The half open door was pushed open wide as a goat came into the hovel. Murdo stood up in surprise.

"She's come to tell me she's needing milked," said Pheemie. "That's a job you could do and save me having to bend down."

He looked at the animal doubtfully. "I don't know what to do."

"It's as easy as can be," she said, getting a bowl. "I'll show you."

The goat's sharp little eyes were fixed on Murdo. He hoped it was only billy goats that butted people.

Murdo made his way to the village to collect his few belongings from the bothy. He left the woods, unaware that two men were following him. Reaching the harbour, they kept out of sight and watched him staring out to sea at the distant fishing fleet. They saw him shrug his shoulders and go along to the bothy.

To Murdo's surprise, he found Alex inside. Before he could question him, Alex was shouting at him.

"Jamie put me off the boat. And it's your fault. They went without me."

"Don't blame me."

"Jamie says I'm bad luck as well as you, because I'm your friend," cried Alex.

"He's not right in the head, him," said Murdo.

"He's not the only one that says it," Alex replied.

Murdo turned away from him. "I can't help what people say."

"You can so."

"How?"

"By keeping away from yon witch," said Alex.

"Folk make up stories about her," Murdo told him.

"Oh aye," said Alex sarcastically. "You're the only one who knows she's not an evil old besom."

"Don't call her that."

"It's what she is. I've lost my job because she's got you in her power," Alex retorted.

"That's blethers," said Murdo. "I'm sorry you got put off the boat."

"I'm sorry you're my so-called friend," said Alex bitterly. "All you do is think of yourself."

"That's not true," Murdo protested.

"It is so," Alex shouted. "You're just a selfish pig."

The sudden sound of the forbidden word halted them. Each looked around frantically for something iron to touch. Murdo clutched a pot and Alex the poker.

"Cold iron!" they cried, and then launched themselves at each other.

They wrestled, and were soon rolling on the floor. Their fight was scrappy. Both knew the other too well to land any real blows, making them frustrated and even more angry. When the door burst open they were yelling in each others face.

Tam and Rab viewed the pair and then pulled them apart. Each held on to his victim tightly. The boys' struggles and protests were no use.

"What's all this?" said Tam. "I thought you were friends?"

"Let go, you've got no right ..." Murdo shouted.

Tam grinned. "We've the laird's right, son. That's all we need. It seems he's wanting a word with you two."

5

Murdo and Alex were left locked in a cellar deep under the castle. If the laird's aim was to terrify them, he had succeeded. Both were tormented by wondering what was going to happen to them. Sir Robert had the reputation of being a cruel man and their fate was in his hands. They had grown up on the horror stories that people enjoyed telling. Tales of torture and death were exciting when they were about other people. And like everybody else, they were familiar with the mutilations that were carried out as punishment for petty crimes. Branding, the loss of an ear or nose, were common penalties. Murdo could only think that the laird was getting his revenge for his telling the Bailie about Pheemie. He felt guilty that Alex was being punished as well.

"Why are you not angry with me?" Murdo cried, as they lay crouched together on the damp stone floor.

"It wouldn't help nothing," said Alex.

"You were angry in the bothy."

"Aye, I was. It was that damned witch."

Murdo groaned. "I wish she *had* bewitched me and I could do a spell to get us out of here."

"Maybe she has, but you don't know about it," said Alex. "That's what folk are saying. Maybe you *could* do a spell."

"Don't be daft."

"Could you not give it a try?"

"Stop talking about it," Murdo grumbled miserably.

He put his head in his hands and closed his eyes. It

was impossible not to be frightened. If only there was some magic that would put the clock back ... All prisoners must feel the same. Like him and Alex, praying for some miracle to end their suffering.

Alex touched his arm. "Listen," he whispered.

A sound came from the door. The key was being turned in the lock. They waited, their eyes glued on the doorway. And then, the door slowly opened.

Paralysed with fear, they watched and waited.

Nothing else happened.

After what seemed like an age, they exchanged looks and stood up.

"What are we to do?" whispered Alex.

"I don't know," said Murdo. "Maybe it's a trap."

"Why?"

Murdo shrugged.

Tentatively they crept to the doorway. Peeping out, they saw nobody. The passage was clear. Holding on to each other, they walked out of their prison.

There was only one way they could take along the passage. It was dark and they felt their way up a spiral staircase. At the top daylight shone in through an open doorway from the castle courtyard.

As soon as they stepped outside, a stinking fishing net fell over them and trapped them in its meshes. Loud laughter greeted their struggles to escape.

"Braw herring, these," shouted Tam, hauling on the net.

"Aye, a fine catch and no mistake," agreed Rab.

The laird and two or three other men were enjoying the scene. Sir Robert called out to the boys. "Caught like a couple of fish. Now you know what they feel like."

Murdo and Alex felt the net tighten around them. They were at the laird's mercy. He regarded them with interest. "You are perhaps wondering why I invited you to come to the castle," he said.

The men laughed.

Sir Robert jabbed his finger into Murdo's chest. "I've been wanting a word with *you* for some time."

Murdo tried to speak, but his mouth was dry and all he managed were a few choked sounds.

"As for your friend," Sir Robert went on, "I have a use for him. Indeed, for both of you. Good fortune has smiled on you," he told them. "From now on you will be working for me." He grinned at the trussed-up boys. "Of course, I realize that may not be your first choice for employment, which is why I arranged for you to have a taste of what will happen to you if you refuse, or try to escape. Am I to take it that you agree?"

Alex spoke. "What do we have to do?"

"Ah — he's interested!" said Sir Robert to the laughing men. "Row a boat, my boy. Something you are both skilled at, I know. The perfect job for a couple of fisherlads. Work well, and you will be rewarded. You've had a taste of the punishment that awaits you if you do not. Agreed?"

The boys nodded their heads.

"Excellent," said Sir Robert. "We have a couple of willing volunteers. Release them," he ordered.

Pheemie walked to the village. Why had Murdo not returned yesterday with his things, as he'd said he would? She had waited all day and had not been able to sleep at night, worrying about him.

When she reached the harbour the fishermen were unloading their catch. It had been a good haul. Some were loading boxes onto carts and others were taking fish to a group of lassies busy gutting. Pheemie kept her distance, knowing there might be trouble if she got too close. Mothers called to their children to keep away from her, but she paid no attention to them.

She peered around, trying to see Murdo in amongst all the activity. She had to find him. The thought of losing her only friend upset her. Once again, unfamiliar feelings had taken hold of her and there were tears on her cheeks. Surely he couldn't have run away? He'd told her he would come back — that he wanted to stay with her.

Looking up from his nets, John Reekie, the Bailie, saw the old woman and frowned. Having her around was not good. However he thanked the Lord she had not been there before the boats went out. That would have meant cancelling the day's fishing. He went up to her.

"And what will you be wanting here, Pheemie?" he asked.

"I'm looking for the laddie called Murdo," she told him.

He grunted suspiciously. Though not as prejudiced as Jamie Findlay, he did not like the idea that the lad had become familiar with the witch. "And why would that be?" he said.

"I need to speak with him."

"I doubt he's busy doing other things. You'd best be on your way."

"Have you seen him?" she asked.

"No," he told her firmly. "And I'd advise you to leave him alone."

"I can see him if I want to."

"And I say you can't," he responded. "As Bailie it's my duty to keep good order here."

"And what is that supposed to mean?"

"That the likes of you don't have a bad influence on our young folk," he told her.

Pheemie tossed her head and pointed at Jamie Findlay working with his crew. "He's the bad influence here. He put Murdo off his boat."

"That's his business. He's the skipper."

"Aye, and his head's stuffed full of superstitious nonsense."

"Away you go now," he told her. "I don't want any trouble." Then, seeing the tears in her eyes, he softened a little. "I expect Murdo is away looking for a job."

"He's got another job," said Pheemie. "Working for me."

He looked at her in amazement. "What do you mean?"

"Just that," she went on. "He's going to be helping me."

John Reekie shook his head doubtfully. "That is not a good idea Pheemie. Folk won't like it."

She snorted. "It's nothing to do with them."

"You know fine you've got a bad reputation in these parts ..." He put up his hand to stop her interrupting. "As I said, you're a bad influence. People won't stand for such an arrangement. They'll believe you bewitched the laddie and there will be hell to pay. I can't allow it. I saved you once, but I doubt I could do it a second time."

"Look at me, Bailie," Pheemie said to him, in tears of frustration. "What harm have I ever done you? Or anybody else? Tell me. Give me proof. It's all gossip. Folk pick on me. Can you imagine what that's like? To spend your whole life being treated worse than a leper."

The Bailie did not want to argue with her, not least because it was difficult to answer her questions. He cursed to himself. People were gathering round them — exactly what he'd hoped to avoid. Like them, he believed she was a witch, but he could not support the vengeance always demanded by the crowd. He spoke to Pheemie, trying to be patient with her. "You cannot deny there have been devilish ongoings of late. And seemingly they are all to do with you."

"Blethers," she spat out. "I'm no more a witch than yon pig that frightened you all half to death."

The cry of 'cold Iron' rose from the crowd, and the Bailie himself hastily touched a nearby bollard.

"Look at you," she went on. "Frightened like bairns."

"Aye, and with good reason." It was Jamie Findlay's voice that answered her. He had joined the crowd. "We live our lives as our forebears did. They understood the ways of good and evil and how to deal with them. And they knew how to deal with the likes of you as well."

"By picking on somebody they didn't like and blaming them for everything," Pheemie told him.

Jamie spoke to the rest of the crowd. "Listen to her. Setting herself up like she knows better than the Town Council and the Kirk. This old baggage would have us disbelieve them."

The Bailie was worried Jamie would incite the crowd. "That's enough, Jamie. We all know your views."

"What *we* would like to know are *your* views, Bailie," Jamie responded. "You were elected to carry out the wishes of the folk here. And they want rid of the witch. I think it's time you did your duty."

There were cries of approval from the crowd. The Bailie knew he had to take action. Though he was the appointed magistrate, he knew little about the law. The only thing he was sure of was that there had to be proof an accused person had committed a crime. Simply believing someone was guilty was not enough. And that was the problem. For all their righteous indignation, he knew there was nobody in the crowd who had proof that Pheemie was a witch.

He spoke to her gruffly. "You'll come along with me."

"Why should I?"

"I'm taking you to the tolbooth," he told her, much to the satisfaction of the crowd.

Pheemie stamped her foot. "I've done nothing wrong. You've got no right to put me in the jail."

"You're creating a disturbance," said the Bailie.

To his relief the crowd let him lead her away, jeering at her protests. Even Jamie Findlay seemed content with his decision. In fact John Reekie had decided to lock-up Pheemie for her own safety. Proving her guilt was a problem for another day. At least he had quietened things down for the moment.

Murdo and Alex pulled on their oars and the boat seemed to skim across the moonlit sea. Behind them the low hills of the Fife coastline were as black as coal. At night it seemed like another world.

"You'll see a difference when we're loaded down," said Tam. He was seated between them, a hand on the end of each of their oars, rowing with them. Rab was at the tiller. A second boat followed, also with a crew of four.

Their target was a twin-masted Dutch barque, anchored half a mile off the sandy cove the smugglers used as their base.

Both boys were excited, in spite of the fact they had been forced to work for the laird. Smuggling was considered a worthwhile trade along the coast and nobody troubled about breaking the law. The King's Excisemen were regarded as figures of fun and they rarely caught anybody landing contraband.

Murdo's only concern was that he had not been able to tell Pheemie what had happened. In a way he'd let her down. But she must see he was better working as a seaman, than in her garden.

They shipped their oars as they drew alongside the Dutchman. Rab threw fenders over the side and they bumped the larger vessel. Tam tied off the mooring ropes dropped down by the Dutch crew. The barque and the small boat rose and fell in the strong swell.

A gibbet-like device was swung out from the Dutchman, for lowering the goods down to the smugglers' boat. The boys heard orders being shouted in a strange language and the sound of crates and barrels being shifted on the deck. There was a creaking of the pulley on the gibbet arm and a barrel came dangling towards them. The closer it got to the small boat, the more it swung on its rope, like a pendulum. It had to be caught and steadied at just the right moment.

"Now!" called Tam, and he and Rab grabbed the barrel. The heaving of the boat made it difficult for them to stay on their feet, but they managed to get the barrel stowed away safely.

"The crates are the worst," Tam told the boys. "They seem to have a life of their own."

Rab nodded wisely. "The trick is not to let it do what it wants to do," he added.

The boat soon filled up with contraband and sat low in the water.

"What d'you think, Tam — another wee barrel of brandy?" asked Rab.

"Aye," he said and shouted up to the deck. "Come on, you two," he told the boys. "You can get this one."

Murdo and Alex had to stand on the already loaded goods. Both were nervous. There seemed no way of knowing when the boat was going to rise or fall. They hung on to each other until the pitching barrel was level with them. They snatched at it and clutched with all their strength. For an awful moment it seemed they were swinging clear of the boat, but the rising swell brought their feet back on board.

However they were unable to steady the barrel's momentum and it swung out over the sea. Both of them cried out in panic. Suddenly Murdo felt his friend let go and fall into the sea. Still clinging on, Murdo swung back and Tam caught him round the waist and Rab grabbed the barrel.

The Dutch crewmen threw a line to Alex, but he couldn't see it as he struggled in the water. Murdo screamed at Tam and Rab, and they thrust an oar over the side for Alex. They could not reach him. Murdo cried out in fear and frustration — Alex was going to drown. The swell was tossing him about like a cork. In one mad moment he was thrown higher than the boat — in the next, he was dropped into a trough below it. The Dutch crew watched helplessly. Tam and Rab yelled at the second boat to come alongside, but the rowers could not control their approach against the tug of the swell.

Murdo was in despair. There was nothing he could do. It seemed wrong to be holding on, fearing for his own safety, when he should be saving Alex. Both boys could swim, but surviving in this swell would be impossible. He let go of the gunnel and stood on a crate. Tam shouted to him to get down and hang on. But he wouldn't. The boat pitched up and the slack rope from the gibbet hit him in the face. He caught it in his hands and in desperation tied it round his waist. He tugged the rope and shouted up to the Dutch crew. Then, glimpsing Alex, he jumped into the sea.

The water hit him hard and winded him. It rushed around his body and would have swallowed him forever, if the Dutch men had not taken the strain on the rope. The salt stung his eyes, but he forced them open. He had to find Alex. His friend was nowhere to be seen. Spluttering water, he called out. Then something wrapped itself around his legs. Immediately he tried to kick out, but he couldn't get free. Nightmare thoughts of sea monsters panicked him. He screamed and pulled on the rope. Slowly it hauled him up, but the terrible thing was still hanging on to him.

It wasn't until he cleared the water that he realized it was Alex who was clinging to him. Murdo shouted to him. All he could do was pray that Alex would be able to hold on. He swung about crazily on the end of the rope until there was a sudden thump. Alex's body had hit the side of the boat.

Murdo felt his friend's hands let go of his legs. But Alex didn't fall back into the sea. Tam had grabbed him and he and Rab hauled him on board. As Murdo crashed down beside them, utterly exhausted, he heard the Dutch crew cheering. He gave an enormous shiver and vomited seawater, before he passed out into blackness.

The next thing he heard was the crackling of a fire. Opening his eyes he saw they were back on the beach. Alex was asleep beside him and Rab and Tam were flopped down on the sand. Not only had they had to row back, they'd also had to unload the cargo.

Murdo shivered and turned his back to the warmth. Some parts of him were dry, others were damp and cold.

"I'm glad to see you're not dead," said Tam. "I couldn't lift another thing." He pointed at the barrels and crates. "You two can carry this lot up the cliff path. The carts will be here afore long."

Murdo said nothing and gave another shiver.

"Take a drop of this," said Rab, passing him a tot of brandy.

Sniffing what it was, Murdo was doubtful. "I've never took a drink afore," he said.

"It'll warm you up."

Murdo sipped the brandy and felt it go down to his belly. Then he choked. He seemed to be on fire.

The men laughed. "It needs a wee bit getting used to," said Rab.

Tam nodded at Alex. "You saved your friend. Mind, you were damned stupid. You could have lost your own life."

"Aye," agreed Rab. "If a man goes overboard, it's his lookout. The rule of the sea."

Murdo nodded. He knew it well enough. The fishermen said the same. But he didn't care. He'd had to go in after Alex and for some reason he had been lucky.

6

Bailie John Reekie walked through the dark streets to the tolbooth. He had decided to release Pheemie and had waited until nighttime to avoid trouble. Quite simply he did not know what to do with her. He'd consulted the minister and been told that the church was becoming wary of prosecuting witches. Too many of those involved in bringing the women to trial had been found to be tricksters, out for their own gain. If the council took action against Pheemie, he would not be able to give his support.

John was left in an impossible situation. He could not bring Pheemie to trial without proper evidence, even though that was what the townsfolk wanted. Without the authority of the church a trial for witchcraft would be a mockery.

John had brought a tinderbox and flint with him. He lit a candle and went downstairs to the cell. Several rats scuttled away from where Pheemie was lying on a bed of straw.

"You frightened them," said Pheemie. "We were sleeping."

"I need to speak to you," John told her.

She sat up, rubbing her eyes. "You picked a queer time to do it, Bailie."

"Maybe. But it's important. I've brought a document for you to sign."

"I can't write."

"You can make your mark," said John.

"I can't read, neither. How do I know what it says?"

"I'll tell you," he went on. "Just listen. This is a legal document made up by the Town Clerk. It says you promise not to behave in such a manner that will alarm and upset the folk of this town. From now on you give your word to be of good behaviour. Do you understand?" Pheemie frowned. "If you agree you can go free. Well?"

"Does it mean you don't think I'm a witch any more?"

John Reekie sighed. "It means you're getting the benefit of the doubt."

She snorted. "You still don't believe me."

He lost his temper with her. "Damn it woman, if you're not a witch, why carry on behaving like one?"

"I don't," she answered. "It's just what folk say about me."

"So you tell me. But it seems to me there's never smoke without fire."

"Blethers," she retorted.

"Do you not see it's dangerous?" he insisted. "It could cost you your life. Are you not feared?"

"Aye, I'm feared," she told him. "But I'll never give nobody the satisfaction of seeing it."

John regarded her. As a fisherman he'd seen bravery at sea. But he had hardly expected to find it in a frail old woman. "I'm not here to argue with you," he said, holding out the document. "Will you sign this?"

She shrugged her shoulders. "I might as well. I'll be glad to get back to my own bed."

"I'm warning you, you cannot treat this lightly," he told her. "If you don't abide by this document, you will be breaking the law and will be punished."

"There's no need to go on. How do I make my mark?"

He took an inkhorn and quill from his pouch. He dipped the quill in the ink and gave it to her. Pheemie made a cross and he wrote under it.

"What's that you're writing?" she asked.

"I'm saying it's your mark," he said. "You can go now. But remember, you have promised to be of good behaviour."

With an effort Pheemie struggled to her feet. "I wish my old bones would remember to be of good behaviour," she grumbled.

A few days later a soft tap-tap sounded on Pheemie's door. She gave a chuckle and opened it. A jackdaw was standing on the step with its head cocked, looking up at her.

"And what might you be wanting?" she asked.

The bird jumped up and settled on her arm, producing an angry miaow from inside the hovel.

"Wheesht, Snowball. He's our friend." Pheemie examined the jackdaw's leg, which it had broken as a chick. She had taken care of the bird until it had mended. "You should be away by now and starting a family," she told it.

She took the bird outside and fed it some grain. Within moments the cock and hens also gathered round. A hedgehog and a couple of rabbits appeared. Then, with a flutter, two nervous woodpigeons landed, followed by a bunch of chattering starlings.

Pheemie sat on a log and spoke to the jackdaw again. "Why are you not up aloft, flying around? I would be if I was you." Often in her dreams she flew like a bird. As a witch, that was what she was supposed to be able to do. Which only showed the ignorance of people.

Not far away Murdo was on his way to Pheemie's hovel. It was a week since he'd last seen her and he was anxious to explain why he had not been able to come back. To his surprise, there was someone else on the path. A man — just up ahead. Murdo followed him and saw him hide himself in a cluster of bright yellow

gorse bushes close to the hovel. A glimpse of his face
told Murdo it was Jamie Findlay.

Murdo didn't know what to do. If he carried on, Jamie
would see him and know where he was going. Then he
realized it didn't matter. He had nothing to do with the
man any more. But he wondered what Jamie was doing,
hiding himself. Murdo could only think that he was spying on Pheemie for some reason. He decided to go on and
warn her. He didn't care if Jamie saw him.

He heard her voice as he approached and found
Pheemie sitting on her log, talking to the animals.

"I thought you'd forgotten me," she said to him.

"I've got a job. On a boat." He didn't want to tell her
he was working for the laird, knowing she would disap-
prove. Hoping she wouldn't question him, he handed
her a twist of paper. "I got this for you," he said.

She held it to her nose. "Snuff," she said. "How did
you know I like a pinch of snuff?"

"I just guessed," he said, sitting beside her.

Pheemie unscrewed the paper and tapped a little
snuff onto the back of her hand. Then she sniffed it up
her nose and sighed. "Grand. Would you like a wee sniff
yourself?"

He shook his head. "I had a drink of brandy last
week," he said, pulling a face. "How can folk drink that
stuff?"

Pheemie chuckled. "You'll come round to it soon
enough when you're a man."

"I seen Jamie Findlay hiding himself in a bush as I
come by," said Murdo. "I think he's spying on you."

She shrugged. "There's aye somebody having a
peek."

"He put my friend Alex off his boat as well, because
of me knowing you," he told her.

Pheemie snorted. "Glaiket Jock's not the only daft

one round here. I told you — fishermen are worse than bairns."

The jackdaw flew up onto Pheemie's arm and let Murdo stroke its head with his finger.

"Where is he — Jamie Findlay?" she asked.

"In the gorse bushes."

She nodded. "He should be able to see us fine from there."

Murdo was puzzled. "You mean you *want* him to see us?"

"Aye, I do," she said. "It's time you got your own back on that awful man. You do what I tell you, and we'll scare the breeks off him."

Talking to animals was all very well, Jamie thought to himself, but he needed more that that. He tried to ease himself into a comfortable position. Bits of the bush seemed to prod his backside whatever he did. He grunted. He'd been right about the boy — he was hand in glove with the witch. He prayed he would get enough evidence to condemn her forever.

Pheemie had stood up. Jamie watched, wondering what she was going to do. The jackdaw was perched on her shoulder and she was holding a staff. She began to move slowly and deliberately backwards. Jamie's belly tightened. Was she doing a spell? She stopped in a small clearing and with her staff she began making out a shape on the ground.

Breath hissed out of Jamie. That's what witches do — make magical signs. Everybody knew that. He followed her every movement. When she had finished, she stood in the centre of the shape she'd created.

Jamie was so tense he would not have been surprised to see her rise up in the air. He began to worry about what he might witness. But he couldn't escape now without giving himself away. He said another prayer.

Pheemie beckoned Murdo and stood him in front of her, placing her free hand on his shoulder. Then they turned in a circle.

What happened next both terrified and perplexed Jamie Findlay. Murdo was facing in his direction, with Pheemie hidden behind him. Suddenly Murdo thrust his arm up and pointed at the sky. "Pigs will fly!" he yelled. Jamie looked upwards to see what Murdo was pointing at. When he looked down again — the witch had vanished. Only the boy was there, holding the staff and with the jackdaw on his shoulder.

Pheemie whispered from where she was hiding in the undergrowth. "Well done, son. Now away you go and do what I told you."

Murdo went to the path and walked along it to Jamie's bush. He stopped and looked around. "I can't see nobody, Pheemie," he said to the jackdaw. "Why don't you have a fly about to see if you can find him."

He took the bird off his shoulder and it fluttered upwards. At the same time a terrible noise came from Jamie's bush. Like a hunted animal in fear of its life, Jamie burst out and charged down the path with a face as white as flour.

To Murdo's delight, the jackdaw flew after him. Pheemie's plan had worked like magic. He'd got his revenge on Jamie Findlay. He couldn't wait to tell Alex. He turned back towards the hovel. Pheemie was on her log taking another pinch of snuff. He grinned. He'd bring her some tobacco the next time he came.

"That'll learn him to keep his nose out of other folks business," she said, and then sneezed. "My, this is good snuff."

"How did you get the idea to trick him like that?" Murdo asked her.

"It was the jackdaw put it in my mind," she said. "Stupid folk say I can fly, so it seemed just right for Jamie."

"Do you want me to see if there are any eggs?" he said.

"Aye, that would be a help."

As he was feeling under the hens Murdo realized that they had not only scared Jamie, they had also confirmed his suspicions that Pheemie was a real witch.

Jamie Findlay knew he looked foolish on horseback. In happier days he'd often admitted he hardly knew one end of a horse from the other. But his mission was vital. He had no choice but to suffer his indignity and get to the castle as soon as possible.

He was sweating and felt sick when he finally dismounted in the courtyard. The groom who took his horse sneered at his incompetence. The laird's butler was equally dismissive. Mere fishermen did not come banging on the door to see Sir Robert.

When he was shown into the study, his knees buckled and he had to be put in a chair.

"God save us," said Sir Robert. "What brings you here in such a state? Findlay, isn't it?"

Jamie nodded. "Aye, sir. If I could just have a wee drop of water ..."

It was provided and the laird waited. "Well?"

Jamie took a deep breath and held on to the side of his chair. "I seen the witch, Old Pheemie, turn herself into a bird and fly away," he said.

Sir Robert's heart missed a beat. However he kept his feelings to himself and regarded Jamie doubtfully. "How did this come about?"

Jamie described what he had seen.

"Are you telling me you just happened to be there?"

"No sir, I was there for a purpose," said Jamie. "For to get proof of her witchcraft."

"Proof?"

"I want her prosecuted," Jamie replied. "She's a witch and she's doing the Devil's work. She has to be stopped. All God fearing folk think the same."

"Are you sure of what you saw?" asked Sir Robert. "Tell the truth. Had you been drinking?"

"I am a Christian man, sir, and strong drink has never passed my lips."

Sir Robert felt a flicker of fear. It had to be true. The man would gain nothing by lying. "Why have you come to me?" he asked. "This is a matter for the town council and the minister."

Jamie snorted. "The Bailie won't do nothing. He let her go free out of the tolbooth and the minister's just a mealy-mouthed weakling."

"You say the boy Murdo helped her?"

"I knew he was bad," retorted Jamie. "I had my suspicions about him and I was right."

"What did he do?" asked Sir Robert.

"Let her sit on his shoulder."

The laird gasped.

"When she was changed into a bird." Jamie became agitated and sat forward in his chair. "The thing of it is, Sir Robert, she *seen* me. She knows who I am. She flew after me. God knows what she'll do." His face was creased with worry. He pointed at the window. "She could be out there now, sitting in a tree, waiting on me."

The laird also glanced towards the window, but checked himself. "If she was going to do anything to you, she would have done it by now," he told Jamie. He didn't believe it, but he had to stop the man gibbering.

"She's got to be got rid of," cried Jamie.

"If what you say is true, I agree."

"I swear it is. I seen it. She should be brought to trial and burnt."

Sir Robert shook his head. "It might not be plain sailing. Trials for witchcraft have fallen out of favour. We would need very hard evidence."

"We've got it!" said Jamie excitedly. "You couldn't have better evidence than what I seen."

"It's not enough," said Sir Robert. "Others will need to testify as well. There has to be more than one witness."

"But you could make sure there was a trial, sir," said Jamie. "They'd surely listen to an important man like yourself."

After he had sent Jamie away, Sir Robert sat thinking.

He believed the man. What he'd told him confirmed what he thought himself — that Pheemie had unearthly powers. Hadn't she used them to make a fool of him? Having her found guilty at a trial would be the safest way of getting rid of her. He was frightened to try any other method of disposing of her, especially after what Findlay had just told him.

But the issue was confused by Murdo. He felt instinctively that if he was put on trial with her, there could be complications. A boy would attract sympathy. There could be doubts about executing one, and not the other. It was too risky.

He remembered it was the boy who had informed the Bailie that he had Pheemie at the castle. He cursed. He should have sent him packing, not employed him. But he'd been desperate for oarsmen. And now, to hear that he was still involved with the witch ...

Sir Robert banged his fist on the table in anger. Something had got be done about that damned boy.

7

The great bell of St Giles Cathedral tolled outside Silas Pow's small attic room. But he was deaf to its booming call to the citizens of Edinburgh. There was a thin smile on his face as he re-read the letter sent to him by Sir Robert Abercrombie. It seemed Sir Robert had heard of his reputation as a witch-hunter and was offering him a generous fee for his help.

He regarded himself in his shaving mirror. Some called him ugly, but he cared nothing for physical vanity. He knew he had the soul of a true believer and the righteousness of his mission shone forth from his eyes.

Silas put the letter down. It would not be the first time he had been called to Fife to investigate those involved in witchcraft. He felt his heart swell.

No lesser person than the Principal of Glasgow University had set him on his task. He had heard him preach a sermon and had never forgotten his words: *Thou shalt not suffer a witch to live.* He had devoted himself to this cause. It had not been difficult. The persecution of witches had been at its height when he was a young man. He observed the methods of the so-called prickers and witch-hunters, and eventually became one himself. His special skill was in recognizing what was known as the Witches' Mark on a witch's body.

He shook his head. Ministers of the church were being urged to concentrate more on teaching the Gospels, and less on destroying witchcraft. It exasperated Silas. The

Devil had to be defeated — all else was second to this mighty undertaking.

He picked up Sir Robert's letter with a righteous glow. Sending these terrible women to their death had been his proudest achievement. He relished the thought of going to Fife and condemning another of their kind to the fire.

Tam and Rab sat drinking in a corner of the alehouse. Both had a smile on his face, thinking of the sum of money the laird had promised them.

"Now, the thing of it is, we don't do it till we're well on our way back to the cove," said Tam. "We'd have to do all the rowing ourselves — and that would never do."

Rab gave a rough laugh. "You're right there."

"And the laird says we're to do for the both of them," Tam went on. "Alex would know too much if we only did Murdo."

"Aye, It would be a risk," Rab agreed. He gulped down some ale and wiped his mouth. "So the rumours are true, then? About Murdo being in cahoots with the witch?"

"Seemingly. God knows, it's queer. You'd think he was just an ordinary laddie. Jamie was wise to put him off his boat. He's not daft, the same man."

"True," said Rab. "Mind, you'd have to admit he's turned a wee bit peculiar lately."

Tam lowered his voice. "And I've heard that's not unconnected with the witch, neither."

Rab frowned. "How's that?"

"I'd not put it past her," Tam told him. "I mind what I seen her do," he added with meaning.

"Talk to the Devil, you said." Rab also lowered his voice.

"Aye, that's right," Tam confirmed. "I *seen* her."

Rab licked his lips. "What did he look like, the Devil?" he asked nervously.

"A great big owl," said Tam. "You could see his eyes flashing across the burn."

"God save us," Rab whispered. "Don't tell me no more."

"It's as true as I'm sitting here beside you, Rab."

Solemnly they each took a large swig of ale.

"There's just one thing," said Rab hesitantly. "If Murdo's like ... in her power. Will she not get back at us — after we've done for him?"

"She'll not know it was us," Tam said. "It'll be like he had an accident."

"Are you sure?"

"Of course I am," Tam told him, putting on a confident air. "Anyway, the laird wants it done, so that's that."

"I doubt it is," Rab replied, trying to ignore what was going on in his head.

"Drink up," said Tam. "It's time we got along to the cove. They'll be waiting at the boat."

The boys were in good spirits during their night's work. Murdo's revenge on Jamie had been a triumph and they giggled every time they remembered it. Alex had admitted that Pheemie could not be as bad as he'd thought. She'd taught Jamie a lesson he'd never forget.

Fully loaded from the Dutchman, they made slow progress towards land. Tam was on the tiller and Rab was rowing between the two boys. Slipping his free hand below the gunwale, Tam felt the marlin spike he'd hidden on board. It was still there. It would soon be time to use it. But there was a problem. Seated in their rowing positions, the boys could see him. They would find it very strange if he left the tiller and came towards them. He needed a ploy to distract them.

Tam could see Rab making faces at him, indicating that they should do it now. The plan was that Rab should restrain Alex, while Tam finished off Murdo and slipped his body over the side. Tam would then hit Alex over the head. It had sounded simple when they'd discussed it over their tankards of ale. Tam gripped the marlin spike.

"Hold hard!" he shouted. "Vessel ahead!"

The three stopped rowing and twisted in their seats to face the bow — including Rab.

"Rab, you damned fool!" Tam yelled. "Grab him."

Rab turned round, realizing his mistake. He tried to get hold of Alex, but the slack oar was pressing into his belly and Alex managed to slip free from his grasp.

Murdo also turned back and saw Tam clambering across the cargo towards him. Within a moment, Tam was standing on a crate over him, his weapon raised. Murdo kicked out at the crate and shifted it enough to tip Tam off balance.

"Murdo!" Alex shouted, thrusting out a hand. Murdo grabbed it and Alex helped him along to the bow.

Both men were shouting angrily at each other. It was a situation neither had forseen and now they were faced with their own stupidity.

The boys looked round frantically for weapons, but there was only the cargo of crates and barrels. In desperation, each one lifted a keg of brandy and held it in front of himself.

By now the unmanned boat was tossing in the swell.

"Get on the oars," Tam roared. "We'll be swamped."

"Get on them yourself," cried Murdo. "You'll get no help from us."

"Tam, Tam, what'll we do?" snivelled Rab, terrified.

"You row," Tam shouted at him. "I'll finish these two."

"I can't..." Rab protested, squeezing between the flapping oars.

Tam began to climb over the cargo towards the bow.

"Stay where you are," Alex shouted at him. "We've done nothing to you."

"If you kill us, you'll hang for it," Murdo told Tam in desperation. "What have you got against us?"

"Nothing — I'm doing a job," said Tam, picking his way closer to them.

"You can't murder us in cold blood."

"I'll do anything if the price is right," snarled Tam, lunging at Murdo with his marlin spike.

Murdo cried out and tried to hurl his keg at Tam, but it was too heavy and it simply fell from his hands.

Tam let out an appalling scream. The keg had fallen on his foot. He toppled down in agony and his weapon flew over the side. Alex placed his keg on Tam's chest and sat on it.

Rab could not control the oars and he was being tossed about like a rag doll. Murdo crawled over to him. He grabbed one oar and held on. "Hold the other!" he shouted at Rab. Between them they brought about a little stability in the boat.

Rab looked at Murdo fearfully. "What are you going to do?" he asked.

"I'm not going to row this boat," Murdo shouted back. "Drag that scum up here," he called to Alex.

They hauled the screaming Tam forward and sat him beside Rab. "Now row, the two of you," Murdo ordered.

"I can't," Tam wailed. "My foot's broke."

"Do it, Tam, do it," cried Rab. They've got the edge on us man."

"Because of *you*, you stupid fool," groaned Tam.

Murdo called to Alex. "Stay behind them, I'll get the tiller. Drop a keg on his other foot if he gives any trouble." He heaved on the tiller and set a course for the cove.

When they finally beached the boat, the boys left the two men slumped over their oars and waded ashore. They avoided the cliff path, knowing that Moir's men would be waiting at the top with their carts. After a rough climb, they threw themselves down on the grass to rest. A grey dawn was breaking.

"Why would the laird want us dead," asked Alex, as he got his breath back.

"Don't ask me," said Murdo.

"We've been doing our job fine."

"Aye," Murdo agreed. "What will he do when he hears we've escaped?"

"Do you think he'll come after us?" said Alex.

Murdo nodded. "I should think so. He'll be feared we'll tell on him."

"Then we'll need to hide. Where can we go?"

"I know," said Murdo.

The Reverend Andrew Robertson was already up and dressed as dawn was breaking. He was a gentle man, who liked a quiet well-ordered life and was sometimes guilty of neglecting the needs of his flock. Andrew found it wearisome having to deal with the mostly uneducated members of his small village kirk. He attended to the fire until the peat was glowing red and then drew water from the well. Inside again, he prepared oatmeal for a simple breakfast.

These everyday activities did nothing to calm his agitation, as he waited for Silas Pow to wake up and join him. He remembered the previous day and felt himself colour with humiliation. Without warning, the laird had appeared with Pow and ordered him to investigate the doings of Old Pheemie. Pow had been introduced to him as an expert in identifying witch-craft and they were to work together. And the laird had added that the minister would provide hospitality for Master Pow.

The minister would have preferred to house a rabid dog. Pow was a bigot whose reputation rested on manipulating the ignorance of folk about the super-natural. Their ready belief in superstition had made his task an easy one. Andrew Robertson closed his eyes and prayed for strength to cope with the man.

"Good day, sir," said Silas Pow, coming into the room. "I trust I am not interrupting your devotions?"

"No you are not, Master Pow. You'll take a bowl of oatmeal?"

"Indeed I will. Thank you."

The minister gave a blessing and they sat down to eat.

"I understand you have never had to deal with one of these evil creatures before, sir?" said Pow.

"No, I have not."

Pow shook his head in wonderment. "With the amount of devilry running riot in the land, I find that hard to believe."

"Maybe I have been fortunate," said the minister.

"Or maybe you have not been sufficiently diligent," Pow responded.

The minister stiffened. "I am not aware of any com-plaints about my ministry. The Kirk Session show sat-isfaction with how I discharge my duties."

Pow gave a sour smile. "Then I suggest the Session needs to wake up its ideas."

"Forgive me, sir, but I find that remark offensive," said the minister.

"The truth is often unpleasant to digest, but it must be faced," Pow told him. "Consider this, sir. I am come here under the good offices of Sir Robert, because he finds that you and the council have been remiss. You have failed to take any action about the witchcraft rife in your parish. We should thank God for that good man's effort to rid the community of evil."

"In my view the evil lies in people's minds," the minister told him. "I see it as my duty to eradicate *that,* not a poor old woman they choose to persecute."

"Then you are in error."

The minister stood up, only just managing to keep his anger in check. "You have no authority to judge me, sir. You are not an ordained minister, nor do you have any legal standing that I am aware of."

Silas Pow gave his thin smile, enjoying the other man's bluster. "My authority could not be more to the point. I have rooted out witches across Scotland and put an end to devilry. Parishes have been cleansed because of my work. My qualification for my task here, is the gratitude I have received from hundreds of good Christian folk."

The minister waved this away. "Who were undoubtedly unable to assess, or understand your methods."

"All I can say to that, sir, is that I hope and pray you will come to see the error of your ways."

Shaking his head, Andrew Robertson went to the door. "You must excuse me," he said brusquely. "I have work to do."

"And so do I," said Silas Pow.

8

"You should have known better than to go working for the laird," said Pheemie, watching the boys eating heaped platters of fried mushrooms.

"He would have kept us in his dungeon if we hadn't," Murdo told her. "We had no choice."

She shook her head. "He's an evil man. Not content with robbing folk of their grain, he's smuggling as well."

Alex eyed Pheemie nervously as he ate his breakfast. In spite of all Murdo had told him about her, he still found it hard to believe she was not a witch. She was exactly what he'd always imagined a witch to be like. *And* she had a big black cat. Everybody knew they always had a black cat.

Pheemie spoke to him. "You're a quiet laddie," she said.

Alex felt his face turning red. He nodded.

"I know what you're thinking."

Alex dropped his eyes.

"Don't be feared, I'll not put a spell on you," she said.

"I told him you're not a witch," said Murdo.

"Aye, maybe," she said. "But it takes a wee bit of believing, does it not, Alex?"

He nodded.

Pheemie went through the slow procedure of filling her pipe and lighting it. "So, you truly don't know why the laird wanted to do away with you?" They shook their heads. "It's queer. For all the man is bad, he's not a fool. There must be a reason."

"What do you think we should do?" said Murdo.

"By rights you should tell the Bailie," she replied. "He's the magistrate. It's his job to stop folk breaking the law."

"But everybody knows fine the Laird does what he wants," said Murdo.

"Aye, and it's time somebody put a stop to him."

"*We* can't," Murdo protested.

Pheemie spoke to Alex. "This is when I wish I *was* a witch. I'd put such a spell on that man, he'd wish he'd not been born."

"All we can do is hide," said Murdo. "But I doubt we can stay here."

She nodded. "He'd find you soon enough."

"We'll need to go away somewhere," said Alex.

Pheemie looked at him and chuckled. "So you *can* speak."

Before Alex could reply, Snowball miaowed and went to the door. Pheemie spoke to the cat. "Aye, I heard." She got up. "Somebody's coming," she told the boys.

"They can't have found us already," cried Murdo.

"Stay in here," said Pheemie and went outside with Snowball.

A man was standing on the path and Pheemie was glad to see he wasn't carrying a weapon. He was dressed all in black and appeared to be a timid soul. Then she realized it was the minister and the surprise took her breath away.

They stood looking at each other. Andrew Robertson spoke first. "Forgive this intrusion, mistress. But I must speak with you."

"I doubt you've not come to ask why I was not at the kirk on Sunday," she said.

He shook his head. "No. Though you would always be welcome."

"That's blethers, and well you know it."

He went on. "What I have to tell you concerns your safety."

She interrupted him. "If this is another of the Bailie's ploys to make me behave myself ..."

"It's nothing like that, I assure you," he told her. "This is extremely serious. The laird is determined to bring you to trial as a witch. And to this end he has employed someone to test you. A man so prejudiced against you, he will not rest until you are found guilty."

Pheemie opened the door of the hovel. "Did you hear that?" she called to the boys. They came outside and stood awkwardly in front of the minister. Pheemie explained their presence to him. "More of the laird's mischief for you, minister."

Andrew Robertson was shocked and questioned the boys. "Is this true — they tried to murder you at Sir Robert's behest?"

"Aye, sir," said Murdo.

"No doubt about it," said Alex.

The minister gasped. "I am appalled."

"It's likely he'll be coming after them," said Pheemie. "And me too, seeing what you've just told me."

"Mistress Pheemie, do you mind if I sit down?" said Mr Robertson, clearly shaken.

She led him to the log.

"Thank you," he said.

"I think I'll join you," said Pheemie, sitting beside him.

The boys exchanged a grin at the sight of the strange pair, side-by-side on the log.

The minister spoke. "What you have told me confirms in my mind that something has got to be done about Sir Robert."

Pheemie sniffed. "The cat could have told us that," she said. "The trouble is there's nothing ordinary folk can do to stop him."

"I've been thinking about that and I think there is something we can do," he replied. "First, I suspect that the laird's witch hunter will be operating without a warrant."

"What's that?" Murdo asked.

"It is the authority from His Majesty's Justice Department required to put a suspect to the test."

"They stick great long pins into you," said Pheemie with a shudder.

The minister nodded. "That is correct. In my view, it is torture." He went on. "Second, for a witch trial to proceed, the commissioners have to be appointed by the Privy Council. My impression is that Sir Robert is not aware of that. So if a trial went ahead without the approval of the Privy Council, it would be illegal."

"Maybe so," said Pheemie. "But who would know?"

"Nobody would, not in a wee place like this," said Murdo.

"The laird is the Lord High and Mighty round here," Alex added.

"That is why I intend to write to the Lord Advocate in Edinburgh," said the minister. The three looked at him blankly. "He is the highest officer of the law in the land," he explained. "If he finds what Sir Robert is doing is illegal, he will stop the trial."

"Can you do that?" said Pheemie doubtfully.

"I can indeed," he replied. "And I shall certainly refer to the laird's conspiracy to murder, as well."

"Will they put him in the jail?" said Alex eagerly.

Andrew Robertson smiled. "It's possible," he said. "But before we arrive at that happy event, there are many difficulties to be overcome. Without doubt the hardest of these is how I can get my letter to Edinburgh."

"There's a mail coach takes letters," said Murdo.

"That would be far too risky, I'm afraid. Sir Robert has his spies. Knowing I was writing to the Lord Advocate would immediately arouse his suspicions."

"Is there nobody you could trust to take it?" Pheemie asked.

The minister shook his head. "Nobody that I can think of," he said.

There was a gloomy silence and then Murdo spoke up. "*We* could do it — me and Alex. We've got to go away from here anyway, so the laird doesn't get us."

"Go to Edinburgh?" said Alex in astonishment.

"Aye. We've seen it often enough, out fishing on the Forth," Murdo told him.

"That would be splendid," said the minister.

"I'm not right sure how we get there, though," said Murdo.

"There's a public coach twice a week that meets the Leith packet boat at Kirkcaldy," said the minister. "I've used it myself. You could take that, and once in Leith it's only a few miles up to the city. You can hire a ride. I will give you money."

Pheemie looked concerned and spoke to the boys. "It's an awful long way. I'm worried for you."

"We'll be all right," said Murdo. "And if it helps us get back at the laird it'll be well worth it."

"They're good laddies, minister," said Pheemie. "I just hope they'll be safe."

"It'll be safer than staying here," said Murdo.

"From what you've told me, that's probably true," said the minister. "However, there remains the question of *your* safety," he told Pheemie. "If you stay here, I'm sure they will take you into custody to wait for your trial."

"You'll have to hide, Pheemie," said Murdo.

"Where can I go, an old body like me?"

"You can't let them take you!"

"Och, I've been in the tolbooth afore," she retorted. "It'll not be for long, if you get the trial put off."

The minister shook his head. "No, no, that would be a terrible risk. We don't know how long it will take the authorities in Edinburgh. The trial could start before we hear."

"What can we do?" Murdo asked the minister.

The minister got up and paced up and down the garden. The others watched him, apparently deep in thought. Eventually he stopped and addressed them. "As you know, I live in the manse. Behind it, in the yard, there is a stable — unused now, since I do not have a horse. You could hide in there," he told Pheemie. "It would be easy for me to get food out to you. There is one hazard, however. I have been obliged to accommodate Silas Pow, the witch hunter I mentioned. But if we take care, I'm sure you will not be discovered. In fact, it could be fortuitous. Nobody will think of looking for you at the manse."

"You'll be safe there, Pheemie," said Murdo.

Pheemie was silent, and then she spoke to Mr Robertson. "There's something I don't understand, minister. Why are you wanting to do this for me? The church has aye disapproved of me, and yet here you are wanting to help me. Why is that?"

The minister weighed his words before replying. "Because I think you are being persecuted. I do not believe in witchcraft. Those who *say* they practise it are poor deranged individuals who are fooling themselves, as much as other people."

"You don't think I'm a witch?"

"You have the misfortune to be old and deformed," he went on. "In their ignorance, folk pick on you for their own selfish reasons. My dearest wish is to restore both them, and you, to the proper meaning of the Christian faith."

Pheemie looked at him in surprise. "And I always thought you could see me far enough!"

The minister nodded sadly. "I have been lax in my duty. I have allowed myself to be swayed by the views of my congregation. I may say the sudden arrival of this cursed witch hunter has been a sharp lesson to me. I intend to make up for my neglect."

"It's a fine sunny morning," said Silas Pow. "Could we not step outside and talk?"

Jamie Findlay shook his head vigorously. "No sir. It is not safe. She could strike at any moment."

They were in Jamie's small cottage, sitting so close together their knees were almost touching. Silas was impressed by Jamie's story about Pheemie. Rarely did you get such compelling proof of a witch's black art.

"I won't know peace until she is burnt to a cinder," Jamie went on.

"Amen to that," said Silas. "This stinks of the Devil's filthy work."

"It was me told the laird we should have a witch trial," said Jamie. "She come after me — a big black bird."

"So you said."

"I seen her. I've never been so feared in my life."

Silas studied Jamie. Under other circumstances he might have thought the man mad. His eyes had a wild glint in them and his body was agitated. Though he had heard many first hand descriptions of witchcraft, Silas had never experienced any himself. Always he was obliged to take them on trust. Not that he doubted the supernatural powers of the Devil and his servants on earth. How could a devout follower of the Lord doubt the existence of evil? But there were times when he yearned to see what these others had seen.

"I'm told she lives in the woods," said Silas.

"Aye. She has a hovel. Animals come and talk to her. It's a fearful sight, sir."

"I must confess I was surprised to find that she had not been apprehended. She should be in custody."

Jamie snorted. "The Bailie had her in the tolbooth and then let her out. He's weak and foolish. That's why the laird took action. The Bailie won't do nothing."

"I think I should have a few words with him."

Silas found John Reekie at his boat mending nets.

"Good day to you, sir," said Silas. "I doubt you know my purpose here?"

"Aye. Seemingly the laird has taken the law into his own hands," said John.

"Now, now, Bailie. That's hardly the language I expect to hear from an official of the town council."

"What you expect is no concern of mine, sir," John told him.

"You talk like a man with a guilty conscience, Bailie," Silas replied. "You have failed in your duty and Sir Robert had no choice but to step in. He has the good of the community at heart, even if you do not."

"I've got nothing to say to you."

Silas gave John Reekie the benefit of his thin smile. "But I think you have. For example, why did you put Old Pheemie in jail, only to let her out again?"

John threw down the net he was working on. "There was no proof against her."

Silas shook his head. "Have you never held a criminal on suspicion, Bailie? Surely that's common practice?

Holding somebody until the evidence against them has been collected."

John remained silent. He had released Pheemie because he didn't know what to do. But he was not going to admit that to this weasel of a man.

"I repeat, you failed in your duty," said Silas. "To make amends, I suggest you re-arrest the old woman immediately. And before you protest, I can tell you that I have proof positive that she is a witch."

John regarded him doubtfully. "Are you sure?" he asked.

"As you are experienced in fishing, so am I in investigating witchcraft," Silas told him, "Do your duty. Arrest that woman."

"There," said the minister, stuffing straw into a sack. "These should make a reasonable bed." He padded the sack down with some others.

"That'll be grand, minister," said Pheemie. "It's a fine stable."

"You will be well hidden here in the stall. But I'm afraid you will be rather lonely."

"I'm used to being by myself," she told him. "Never fear, I'll soon make a few friends."

He was startled. "You can't have other people coming here, it's much too dangerous."

"I'm not meaning folk," she replied. "See, there's a swallow's nest up under the roof and I've already seen a mouse or two, skittering about. Don't worry about me. I'll not be lonely."

He regarded her with a smile. "I've heard it said you talk to animals."

"Of course I do," she said. "Though why folk find it strange I'll never know. Don't they talk to their cats and dogs?"

"You're right. I'd never thought of that."

"My hens will still be laying while I'm here. You can go and collect their eggs, if you like. And you could tell Snowball I'll be back as soon as I can."

"Yes, if you wish," he said unsurely. "Now the most important thing is that you are not seen by Silas Pow. Much against my wish, he is staying here. However there should be no reason for him to come into the stable."

Pheemie chuckled. "You could give him a witch's egg for his breakfast," she said.

The minister laughed. "That would be a rare delight," he said. "But seriously, Pheemie, we must take care. They will hunt for you high and low."

"And what about yourself, minister?" she asked.

"What do you mean?"

"It's a terrible risk you're taking, hiding me. And you a man of God."

"That's why I'm doing it," he told her.

"But are people like you not supposed to tell lies?"

The minister frowned. "I do not agree with what Sir Robert and Silas Pow are doing. So you could say I am fighting them with their own weapons."

"Lies, you mean?"

"Exactly," he said.

The Leith packet was the largest vessel Murdo and Alex had ever been on. The snap and crack of the sails and the creaking timbers were new and exciting. Racing across the Firth of Forth they left every other craft in their wake. It was easy to imagine themselves as old sea dogs and they laughed at their seasick fellow passengers. Even though both shores remained in sight, the lads had the feeling they were on the open sea. The slap of the waves on the bow and the spray wetting their faces was exactly how they pictured sailing on a great ocean.

The bosun of the packet kept his eye on the boys. He'd noticed the amount of coins clinking in their purse when they'd paid for their passage. He didn't bother to wonder where two simple country lads had got them from. But he did speculate on the possibility of removing their money from them. It was a golden opportunity if he ever saw one. The daft loons — did they not realize the world was a harsh place?

As the boys stepped off the gangplank they looked around in amazement. The port of Leith appeared like a giant ants nest, such was the bustle of activity that suddenly surrounded them. Vessels of all shapes and sizes were being loaded, or unloaded, and the noise of carts and shouting men was all that could be heard. They stood still, not knowing what to do. The minister had said there were always carts and coaches travelling to Edinburgh, but they could see no sign of a road.

There was a coarse shout and Murdo pulled Alex out of the way of a swearing porter and his barrow. Together they pushed their way across the crowded quay and found themselves outside an alehouse. It too was packed with men and stank of drink and tobacco smoke. No sooner had they stopped, than a man's body crashed between them and fell sprawled on the ground. He was followed by another man who pushed them aside and hauled up the first and began punching him.

Men heaved out to watch the fight and the boys had to hold on to each other to avoid being knocked over. Alex shouted in Murdo's ear and tugged him into the almost empty alehouse. They sat down and Alex used some of the minister's money to buy them a jug of ale.

"We must ask somebody how to get to Edinburgh," said Murdo.

"Aye, but I can't say I like the look of any of the folk round here," said Alex, keeping his hand on the purse hanging from his belt.

"We have no choice. You know we've got to be as quick as we can."

Alex nodded. Like his friend, he disliked having to admit their ignorance of city ways. He took a drink from his mug and saw a man approaching them.

"Well, if it isn't the two fine lads from the East Neuk," said the bosun, sitting down at their table. "Did you enjoy the crossing?"

They nodded.

"I could see you were a couple of hardy sailors," he went on. "I don't mind telling you, it's a torment for most of the folk we get on board. Where are you heading?"

The boys looked at each other. "Edinburgh," said Murdo.

"I see. And what brings you to the city — are you looking for work?"

"No, we ..." Murdo stopped. "We're going to see his gran," he continued. "She stays in Edinburgh."

"Aye," said Alex. "So she does."

"And where might that be?" asked the man.

"What?"

"Which *part* of Edinburgh does your grannie live in?"

Alex looked helplessly at Murdo, who shrugged. "She stays next door to the castle," he said. He'd heard that there was a castle in Edinburgh.

The bosun hid his smile. "I doubt she'll be glad to see you," he said. "How are you going to get there?"

"We're not right sure," Murdo confessed. "What do you think we should do?"

"Get a ride on a cart," the bosun told him. "It's not difficult. As it happens, I know a carrier who sets off in about half an hour's time, from a livery stable. Would you like me to show you where it is?"

"Would you?" said Murdo. "That would be grand."

"Aye," said the bosun. "Finish your drinks and follow me."

Outside the alehouse they were crushed together until the bosun led them down a narrow alleyway off the quay. It soon joined a lane flanked with warehouses and stables. He pointed at a sign further along the lane.

"See, down there. The man's name is Dougie. He'll give you a ride up to the city, no bother." He edged away from them. "Now, I've to be on my way."

Both boys thanked him. But he was already walking off and it's doubtful if he heard them.

Now they knew what to do, their confidence returned and they hurried to the stable. "How much do you think we should pay?" asked Alex.

"We'll need to pay what he asks."

Alex reached for his purse, only to find it was no longer hanging from his belt. "My purse!" he cried. "It's not there. I've lost it."

Murdo looked at the thongs hanging from his belt. They had been cut. "It must have been him."

Alex swore. "How did he do it? I didn't feel a thing."

"Because he's done it before, I shouldn't wonder," said Murdo bitterly.

Alex ran down the lane, but the man had disappeared. "I'll kill him," he shouted angrily.

"Save your breath, Alex, you'd never find him," said Murdo. He felt his jerkin. He thanked God the letter was still tucked safely inside.

"What'll we do?" said Alex, almost in tears.

"Find our way to Edinburgh."

"With no money?"

"There's got to be a way," said Murdo.

9

Striding down to the harbour, John Reekie passed a group of shrieking children. From their cries he realized they were pretending to have a witch burning.

"Burn the witch! Burn the witch!"

He sighed. Even the children — what was the town coming to? He was glad to be getting away for a day's fishing. The men getting their boats ready parted to let him by. And as if by signal, the small groups fell silent. When he reached his boat he saw that his crew was missing. He felt himself being watched and saw that every fisherman was standing staring at him.

His first feeling was one of humiliation. He stood like a fool, not knowing what to do. He knew he could walk away, but that would not satisfy the anger boiling inside him. The men were waiting to see what he would do. That was what it was all about — he was being taunted and tested. And they were hoping he would be found wanting.

Though it was hard to contain his anger, he decided to sit down and wait it out. He'd do nothing. That way, *he* would be testing *them*. And as the minutes passed, it began to look as if his ploy was working. The men grew tired of the silence and some shuffled back to their nets.

"There he is — the witch's friend!" a voice bellowed.

John recognized it immediately — Jamie Findlay.

"Are you not ashamed of yourself, Bailie. How dare you show yourself among Christian folk?"

"So this is your doing, Jamie? I might have known," John shouted back at him.

"It's not just me," Jamie responded. "The whole town's sick of you. Letting the witch go free and now she can't be found. She should be in the jail, waiting her trial. But because of you she's disappeared. We don't want you as Bailie no more."

"If that's what you think, you know what to do about it," John told them. "Vote in somebody else. Myself, I'd nominate Jamie Findlay — the laird's toady. He'd be a fine choice, since the laird rules the roost anyway."

Jamie strode forward angrily. "You take that back."

"If I did that, Jamie, I'd be lying," said John. "And that's a sin, is it not? A Christian man like yourself would surely not want me to be guilty of that."

"Take it back!"

John looked at him. They'd worked together in the fishing fleet since they'd been lads. Jamie was an old friend.

"No."

Jamie sprang at him, catching John by surprise and they both fell over. John wriggled out from under Jamie and got to his feet. But before he could move away, Jamie grabbed one of his legs and pulled him down again. John hit the ground with a sickening thud, hurting his hip and elbow. He cried out and swore.

Jamie gave a gloating laugh and punched John in the belly.

The watching men cheered and helped Jamie up. On his feet again, he kicked John, whose body was aflame with pain. The Bailie had never suffered physical violence, nor yet had to fight a man. Crazily he wondered what he must do to stop it.

Hands lifted him to his feet and he was grateful for their help, until Jamie landed a blow on his chin. He staggered back, then reeled round, desperate for a way to escape. But he was trapped by the crowd of men surrounding the fighters. They were shouting abuse at him as if he was the worst kind of criminal.

Jamie came at him. John swung his arm wildly and felt his fist hit Jamie's face. Jamie yelled in fury, blood running from his nose. From that moment John knew that it was all up. Even if he'd had the energy and strength to fight back, he could never have stopped Jamie. The man had become fanatical and oblivious to pain. He threw himself at John and punched and kicked as though he would murder him.

The men pulled Jamie away and left John lying on the ground. When he came to, he at first was only glad for the peace he felt. His cheek was resting on the stone of the harbour and it seemed as comfortable as a pillow.

Something moved in front of his eyes. There was a shape. Wisely he did not try to raise his head. The shape became a face, lying down beside his own. He heard a nervous giggle. It was Glaiket Jock lying beside him. The boy giggled again.

John tried to speak, but his bloodily swollen lips refused to move. So it was the town daftie who had the last word.

"You should've got the witch to help you, Bailie," said Jock. "They're all feared o' her."

Moir was waiting for Sir Robert Abercrombie in the secluded part of the woods they had chosen for their meeting. Sir Robert dismounted and they greeted each other gruffly. Moir was holding a purse and Sir Robert put out his hand for it.

"You'll find I've had to make a wee deduction," Moir told him.

"What the devil are you talking about?" replied Sir Robert.

Moir shrugged. "Trouble on one of your boats. When it landed, two of your men had disappeared, and one was wounded, and the other was laid low with exhaustion. My men had to unload the boat and carry the goods up the cliff. Naturally they had to be compensated."

"Damn it, you got the goods."

"At the cost of extra time and money."

"They have no right to demand payment," Sir Robert retorted.

"Forgive me sir, but those are the words of someone who has never had to do any manual labour."

"You can keep your insolent remarks to yourself," said Sir Robert, his temper rising.

There was the flicker of a smile on Moir's face. "My men got the impression that the two who made off, were anxious to get away from *you.*"

Sir Robert took a step towards him. "You would do well to mind your own damned business."

"Nothing would give me greater pleasure. But unfortunately its success depends on your efforts." Moir brushed mud from his boots. "I don't wish to be offensive, but this latest episode shows they are not up to snuff."

Sir Robert glared at him. "For the last time, I would remind you who you are dealing with. I will not tolerate such talk from the likes of you. People fear me in these parts. You would do well to remember that."

"I'm well aware of your rank, Sir Robert," sneered Moir. "And I can understand how it must grieve you to have to deal with a mere merchant. Howsoever, I am of a mind to call a halt to our partnership — for the meanwhile, anyway. You clearly cannot handle your part of the bargain."

The laird was speechless with rage as Moir went on.

"Maybe when you have got rid of the witch things

will settle down. Everything stems from her bad influence. Rumour has it that she slipped through your fingers. It seems she's got you dancing to her tune. Imagine that — she a poor old woman, and you the laird that everybody fears."

Moir re-mounted his horse and trotted away. "Good day, Sir Robert," he called over his shoulder.

Silas Pow was at the castle waiting to report to the laird on his return.

"Well?" demanded Sir Robert.

"She has still not been found," said Pow. "In spite of your men's best efforts. They have covered the countryside."

"Damn the woman," cursed Sir Robert, still smarting from his encounter with Moir.

"It defies rational explanation — that an old and infirm woman could escape our attentions." Pow shook his head and went on cautiously. "I fear some diabolical intervention, sir. That can be the only reason."

Shaken, the laird sat down. He glared at the man, as though doubting his words. "You cannot be sure of that."

Pow shrugged his shoulders. "From what we know of her, it seems the most likely. Her master the Devil has helped her to disappear."

"I refuse to believe it," said Sir Robert. But inside himself there was a terrible fear of what Pow was suggesting.

"Sir, she is a witch. Such a thing is possible."

"In your experience, have you encountered such a thing before?"

Pow hesitated. "I have come across similar events," he said carefully.

"Damn it, how similar?" Sir Robert retorted.

"Women who transform themselves into other beings," Pow went on. "Were you to read the transcripts of previous trials you would see it is a skill possessed by these evil women. And Old Pheemie has already demonstrated she is capable of that."

Sir Robert sank back in his chair. He felt like a man who has run full tilt into two stone walls. First Moir, and now Silas Pow. He spoke in a resigned voice. "It seems to me, Master Pow, that you might as well go home."

"We cannot give up now, sir."

"How so? If she has turned herself into somebody else, we will never find her." Sir Robert gave Pow a stern look. "I should have said that much was obvious."

"But the people are expecting a trial," said Pow. "They want rid of the menace."

"Then they will be disappointed."

"Forgive me for saying so, but they expect it of you, Sir Robert. As their laird, you cannot let them down."

Sir Robert stood up in fury. "Nobody wants rid of her more than I do," he cried out.

"I know, sir. And I beg of you to let me pursue my investigation," Pow said hurriedly. "And I make bold to say that with God on our side, we are bound to succeed."

"Then do it!"

"I will find a way, I assure you," Pow told him.

But as the witch hunter left the castle, he faced a problem that did not appear to have a solution. All the fields and crofts and outhouses had been searched. Repeating that again was not the answer. How had she done it? The question tormented him. Somewhere there must be a clue that would help him. Some shred of evidence of what had happened to her — even if it was supernatural. There must be.

Murdo and Alex watched the road to Edinburgh. Mostly there were carts, with a few coaches and the odd person on horseback.

"Can we risk it?" asked Alex.

"We've got to," said Murdo impatiently. "See, there — that one." He pointed at a long low cart being hauled by no less than four horses. "We can get on the back of that. He'll never know."

They waited until the cart had just gone past them and then ran behind it. There was a tailboard, but it was not very high and they were able to grab it and haul themselves up. The cart was full of crates packed round with straw. They pressed themselves into the straw, sure the carter had not noticed them. Grinning at each other, they settled themselves down for a comfortable ride.

"I know you're there," said a voice. It was the carter.

With sinking hearts they scrambled upright, ready to jump off the cart.

"Just hold on," called the carter. "I'll give you a ride. But it'll cost you."

"We've got no money," said Alex.

"I'm not wanting any," replied the man. "You can work for your ride. What d'you say?"

"Aye," cried the boys together.

When they finally halted in Edinburgh they discovered that their work was to unload the cart. It was then that they realized how huge it really was and how many heavy crates had been packed onto it. They were in a builder's yard and the crates had to be unloaded and stacked in an old byre.

"Don't drop them," ordered the carter. "I want nothing broken."

"What's in them?" asked Murdo, as he and Alex struggled with the first crate.

"Floor tiles, for the kitchens of the gentry," he told them grandly. "Look sharp, or it'll be dark afore you're finished. I'd help you myself, but I hurt my back last week."

"How did you do that?" said Alex.

"Unloading crates of tiles," he replied.

Neither of the boys had ever worked harder. It seemed they would never get to the last crate. Darkness fell and the carter grumbled about having to waste oil on lighting a lamp for them. When the task was finally completed, they collapsed onto the straw exhausted.

Cold and hunger woke them up at dawn. Desperate for something to eat, they went into the horses' stable and found a bag of oats. Each took a handful and dipped it in the water trough, then squeezed the oats tight. They were not the best oatcakes in the world, but they made several and ate them with relish.

Cocks were crowing and smoke starting to rise from kitchen fires when they left the builder's yard. They had no idea where they were. Tall buildings rose up on either side of them and once again they had to risk asking for directions. The minister had told them they had to go Parliament Hall, which was near the cathedral of St Giles.

Alex nudged Murdo and nodded at a small boy sitting on a mounting black, dangling his toes in a puddle. "What about him? We can fight him if he tries to rob us."

The boy put his arms up over his head when they approached him.

"We're not going to hurt you," Murdo told him.

"I didn't do nothing," cried the boy.

"We didn't say you did."

"I *didn't*." Tears rolled down his cheeks.

"Here," said Alex, giving him a handful of damp oats.

The boy snatched them out of his hand and stuffed them into his mouth.

"Do you know where we are?" Murdo asked him.

"Embra."

"Aye," said Murdo. "Do you know what they call this bit we're standing in?"

"Embra."

"Does this street not have a name?" asked Alex.

"Aye," nodded the boy.

"What is it?"

"I don't know," the boy answered.

"We're wasting our time," said Alex.

"Do you know the great big kirk they call St Giles?" asked Murdo, at his wits end.

The boy suddenly jumped up and ran along the street.

Surprised, Murdo and Alex quickly ran after him. The street was long and almost empty and the boy scampered as fast as he could go. When he stopped he pointed at the cathedral, and then held out his hand.

Murdo shook his head. "We've got nothing, son."

The boy pointed at Alex's other hand, in which there were still some oats. He grabbed them and ran away.

They crossed the square in front of the cathedral to where a man was sweeping the steps of a large building.

"Where's Parliament Hall?" Murdo asked him.

"You're looking at it," he replied.

10

Silas Pow ate his porridge in silence. This suited Andrew Robertson very well since he had no desire to speak with the man. When Pow had finished his breakfast, he mumbled a grace and left the room without another word.

The minister went to the window and watched him leave the house. Satisfied it was safe to do so, he emptied the porridge pot into a bowl and took it out to Pheemie.

"I never thought I would see the day when I would be waited on by a minister of the kirk," she said, taking the bowl from him.

"Fortunately that awful man never notices that I make more than for two of us," he told her. "He has too much on his mind. Your disappearance has flummoxed him completely."

Pheemie chuckled. "Maybe they'll give up looking for me."

"I doubt that. We certainly need the time. We can only pray that the boys are not delayed. In my experience, advocates do not move quickly."

"Aye, it would be good to know how they're doing."

"How's the porridge? I hope it hasn't cooled down too much."

She shook her head. "It's just fine. Have you been to collect any eggs yet?"

"I'm afraid I've been much too busy," he told her. "Looking for you."

She frowned. "You know where I am."

"*Pretending* to look for you. I'm supposed to be assisting Master Sourpuss Pow."

She grinned at him. "I was forgetting. It was a canny idea — hiding me here. And some more tenants arrived just last night." Pheemie put her bowl down and went to the corner of the stall. She stooped down and very gently lifted some of the straw.

The minister gasped. A mouse was curled up in her nest feeding her newly born family. He wrinkled his nose — the young mice looked no more than blobs of red raw skin. Pheemie said a few quiet words to the mother and replaced the straw. Watching her, the minister realized there was something special about the old woman. She *was* different from other people. Because they had rejected her, she had grown in her own way. Not as a witch, but as someone who had an extraordinary respect for animals, and, magically, they for her.

"You know, Pheemie, I have heard tell of an eastern religion that believes in the sanctity of animals," he said. "It may sound strange to us, but they do not believe in killing them. Not for food, or for any other purpose."

"I doubt it would work in Scotland, minister," she said.

"Sadly, no." He helped her up. "I will go to collect the eggs, I promise."

The old woman's eyes brightened at the prospect of a nice meal to come.

Pheemie's hovel lay in ruins. The men searching for her had vented their anger on her humble dwelling. Silas Pow saw this vengeance as right and proper, as he cast his eye over the wreckage. A witch deserved no mercy.

Tentatively he walked in the garden like a man who has lost something. As he brushed by the flowering herbs, their pungent smells were released and wrapped themselves around him. He halted and mopped his brow. In his mind he saw these unfamiliar plants being used by the witch to make her evil potions. He was fearful of being tainted by her black magic, but he had to steel himself to search for a clue to Pheemie's disappearance. Silas prayed to God that he would find what he was looking for — even though he did not know what it was. Convinced that the witch's lair was the best place to start, he forced himself to continue.

He recognized the smell of mint. There was a large bed at his feet and looking at it he noticed a black shape, half hidden in the leaves. Immediately he became suspicious. It was clearly not natural. He felt a tremor of fear and his palms sweated. Could this be what he was looking for? Now that it seemed he'd found something of interest, he cursed the fear that froze him to the spot. He could not move. Visions of the evil that might overwhelm him filled his mind.

Sweat was running off his brow and into his eyes. He had to wipe them. As he moved to reach for his kerchief, a shrieking black shape suddenly leapt up at him. Claws tore at his hands as he tried to protect himself. He staggered back and fell to the ground crying out in pain.

Snowball stood before him, his back arched and hissing.

Pow jumped to his feet and stumbled away from the cat. His heart was striking hammer blows in his chest and he could not go far. Luckily the cat did not follow him. It stalked away to the ruined hovel, its tail in the air like a triumphal banner.

As he wiped the blood on his hands, a fearful thought struck the witch hunter. Was that her? Had she taken on the form of a cat? Again he froze in horror. He'd lost count of the number of times he'd heard of witches turning themselves into animals. Was he now a witness to such a transformation? He trembled with fear. Silas Pow had the strange sensation that his body was both hot and cold at the same time.

The cat had vanished and he tried to get his breathing back to normal. He had to pull himself together, if only to get away from this awful place. A movement caught his attention, near the ruined hovel. A bird was pecking at the ground. It was a jackdaw and it was strutting about as though it owned the place.

A jackdaw! Instantly Pow remembered that Jamie Findlay had seen the witch become a jackdaw ... He stopped breathing. The bird's every movement seemed like a threat to him. The glint in its eye, the sharp turn of its head, its sleek black feathers, proclaimed to him its evil intent. And then it spread its wings. He clasped his bloody hands in prayer as the bird launched itself up into the air.

What could he do? He dropped to his knees and closed his eyes. Minutes passed and nothing happened. When he risked opening his eyes again, the bird was nowhere to be seen.

Never had he felt so weak and useless. Grimly he recalled how he had yearned to experience the supernatural power of witchcraft. Never again! His earnest wish was to be spared such an experience. But his wish was not granted. At that moment he heard a sound. Something was moving in the woods and coming towards him. He looked round frantically for a hiding place. All he could see was a gorse bush. He scrambled to it and lay beneath it like a hunted

animal. His mind was in turmoil. It might be the
Devil himself, come to consort with his earthly servant the witch. Not daring to look, he heard the sound
come closer and then he identified it. Footsteps, and
they were making their way to the ruined hovel. He
risked looking for the black bird. It would be sure to
come down to meet its master ...

The figure of a man appeared by the hovel. Pow had
the sun in his eyes, but he could see he was dressed all
in black. He whimpered with fear and bit his knuckles.
The man was examining the damaged building. He
looked down. The cat was rubbing itself against his
legs. There was a sound. The man was laughing. Then
Pow saw the cat jump up into his arms. As the man
steadied himself, Pow glimpsed his face. It was the
minister.

Pow felt as if his brain would burst out of his skull.
He could not begin to understand what was going on.

Still laughing, the minister put the cat down and they
both went peering under the bushes near to the hovel.
They disappeared from view, but soon returned — the
minister carefully carrying something wrapped in a
kerchief. He stooped and spoke to the cat and stroked
its head.

Pow tried to add up the astonishing facts he had
witnessed. The witch could change from a cat, to a
bird, and back again. Seemingly, the Devil had taken
on the form of the minister. He could not but wonder at the Evil One's cunning, and it explained why
Andrew Robertson had been reluctant to act against
the witch. He yearned to be back at the castle to tell
the laird what had been revealed to him. But all was
not over. The minister had set off. He must follow him.
Who could tell what other diabolical business he had
in mind?

Pow kept a goodly distance behind the minister, at the same time wishing the man would walk more slowly. His body was full of aches and pains from his ordeal and he was sweating with effort. It soon became clear that the minister was heading back to the manse. When he reached the front door, Pow hung back and waited for him to go inside. After a few minutes he adjusted his clothes and entered the house. It was empty.

Was this more black magic? Pow trembled, but then he caught sight of the minister through the back window. He was going towards the old stable, still carrying his bundle. As soon as he was inside, Pow sneaked out of the back door and tiptoed across the yard. Standing outside the stable he heard the minister's voice.

"Look, Pheemie — see how many I've collected."

Murdo and Alex didn't know whether they were kept waiting a long time, or a short time. A man had taken the letter from them and they were left in the corner of an enormous hall. The splendour of the place and the people moving busily back and forth overwhelmed them. Advocates in their flowing black gowns stalked about like crows scouring a field for grain. Everybody was in fine clothes, making the boys feel like a couple of tinkers' bairns.

"I can't think the Lord Advocate will be fussed with the minister's letter," whispered Murdo. "Not with all these folk to attend to."

Alex was staring at the scene around them with his mouth hanging open. He nodded. "Aye. He'll have more important things to do."

"The minister said he has to look after the whole of Scotland."

Alex nodded again. Their little fishing town seemed a very long way away.

Some time later the man who had taken their letter summoned them to follow him down a corridor.

"Where are we going?" asked Murdo.

"The Lord Advocate wishes to speak to you," said the man, tapping on a door.

The two boys felt their knees go weak.

"I'm sorry, Pheemie, truly sorry," said the minister. "It was my fault. I should have been more careful."

"Wheesht, minister, you're not to say that," she told him. They were both in the tolbooth jail. Pow had lost no time in telling the laird's men where to find Pheemie. They had been doubtful about arresting the minister as well, but Pow had insisted. He told them hiding a witch was a criminal offence. It also gave him particular pleasure to see the man humiliated like some common rogue.

"All I can say is, I will speak up for you," Andrew promised. "Plead on your behalf."

"You're a good man," she said, nodding her head wearily. But in her heart she knew that goodness was a weak weapon against the likes of the laird. All his life he had got what he wanted. Nothing was allowed to stand in his way.

The minister stooped down beside her. "The boys should have reached the Lord Advocate by now. It is not too late for him to take action. We must pray that time is on our side."

"Tomorrow, she goes on trial tomorrow," said the laird.

"I agree," said Silas Pow. "The sooner, the better."

"But what do we do about the minister?" asked the Bailie.

The laird ignored the question. "My good friend the sheriff has consented to chair the commission. As County Sheriff this will give the trial a proper legal standing."

The Bailie shook his head. What Sir Robert really meant was that the sheriff was a deferential old man who would do what he was told by his aristocratic superior. He spoke up again. "Sir Robert, I repeat. We have the minister in the town jail. Such a thing has never happened before."

It was Pow who responded. "Ministers are ordinary citizens and if they break the law they must take the consequences."

The laird agreed with him. However the minister's involvement was a complication he could have well done without. "He will be dealt with separately. When we have finished with the witch."

"Should we not inform the church authorities?" said the Bailie.

"In good time," snapped the laird. "What concerns us now is the witch. Master Pow, tell us how we should proceed."

"Very good, Sir Robert. Essentially the trial must seek to prove that she made a pact with the Devil to become his servant and renounce God and Christian baptism. That is how the law words it. We should commence with the witnesses, those who have seen the witch practise her black arts. There are several who have witnessed her diabolical deeds. Jamie Findlay, Tam Brodie, Master Moir ..."

Sir Robert interrupted him. "I don't want Moir testifying. The man is not to be trusted."

"With respect, sir, the man's character does not matter, it is what he saw ..."

"He is not to be trusted," the laird repeated. "I do not want him to speak."

Silas Pow gave a reluctant sigh. "Very good, Sir Robert," he said. "After the witnesses, I shall conduct the test."

"What's that?" asked the Bailie.

Pow reached into his jerkin and took out a leather wallet. He opened it and revealed a selection of long needles. "The tools of my trade, gentlemen," he told them. "They allow me to discover the Devil's mark on the witch's body — proof positive of her evil doing."

"With needles?" said the Bailie.

"Indeed, Bailie. The operation is called pricking. The needles are inserted into the woman's body. Should she not cry out in pain, or should there be no blood — a Witches' Mark has been located."

The Bailie shuddered. "Surely it must always hurt," he said, eying the length of the needles.

Silas Pow gave his thin smile. "I'm afraid you are betraying your innocence in these matters. I can assure you these creatures are not aware of the needle, even when it is pushed fully into the flesh. It is quite clear that the Devil makes them immune to pain and bleeding."

The laird cleared his throat. "You say she must confess?"

"That is the law."

Sir Robert frowned. "If she feels no pain — as you say — how will she be persuaded to make a confession?"

"I assure you, sir, when confronted by the result of the test, they have little choice."

"But if she does not?" the Bailie insisted.

Silas Pow showed his irritation. "It is most unlikely."

"Even so, we must be prepared," said the laird.

"Of course, sir." Pow put his needles away. "Should she not be persuaded to confess by the pricking, we would be obliged to swim her. That never fails."

"Tell them, in the King's name, they must hold the packet for us," ordered Captain Nicol, dispatching one of his men off at gallop. He turned in his saddle and spoke to Murdo and Alex, who were riding beside him. "Can you not go faster than that?" he demanded. "I swear a couple of milkmaids would make a better job of it than you two."

"We're fisherlads," said Alex. "There's not much need for riding when you're catching herring."

Captain Nicol cursed. "I am ordered by the Lord Advocate to proceed with all possible speed. Now move, blast you," he shouted, whacking the boys' horses.

"God save us!" cried Murdo, as his horse turned its trot into a gallop.

"I don't know which bit to hold on to," Alex called out, sure he was going to bounced out of his saddle.

"That's better," bellowed the captain. "Keep going."

The news that they were to travel home with a troop of the King's Guard had thrilled the lads. Now as they sped towards Leith in the cold light of dawn, they were not so sure. However they were glad to be leaving Edinburgh. The Lord Advocate had questioned them about the smuggling and they had been fearful they would be arrested. But it seemed they'd been let off, and they were anxious he wouldn't change his mind.

The troop of horses made a great clatter as they boarded the packet boat. Murdo and Alex watched them being tethered on the deck. They were glad to be on their feet again.

Murdo nudged his friend. "See who's over there." It was the bosun, showing the soldiers where to put their horses.

"What shall we do?" asked Alex

"Ask him for our money back."

Alex snorted. "He'll pay no heed to that."

"I think he will," Murdo told him. "I've had an idea."

During the crossing, while Captain Nicol was busy being seasick, Murdo was able to have a word with the soldiers. Later, as they were approaching the end of the crossing, Murdo signalled to Alex and they went to find the bosun. He was checking the horses and they immediately began calling him names.

"You great dod of horse dung!"

"You lousy stinking son of a bilge rat!"

The bosun yelled at them and they dodged away, still shouting insults. Furious, the man chased them, but he soon skidded to a halt. He'd suddenly found himself confronted by a solid line of brawny soldiers. Before he could say a word, two of them lifted him off his feet and held him over the side of the boat.

"The laddies want a word with you," he was told.

"Give us our money!" shouted the boys.

The bosun yelled and spluttered as the sea spray drenched him.

"We can't hear you," cried the boys, enjoying themselves.

Laughing, the soldiers hauled the bosun back up and dumped him on the deck. "You'll get your money back now lads."

The boys held out their hands and the bosun hurriedly filled them with coins. And then the captain's voice bellowed across the deck, ordering his men to stand by their horses, ready for landing.

11

On the day of the trial the weather got steadily worse. The wind rose early in the morning and was soon joined by lashing rain. The townsfolk blamed the witch. It was her revenge for being caught and put on trial. Fishermen struggled to beach their boats far from the angry sea. Buildings were shuttered and children forbidden to go outside into the storm.

All along the north coast of the Firth of Forth was affected and the troop of horsemen found themselves battling against the terrible conditions. The road was slippery with mud and shallow fords became deep and treacherous. The captain urged his men on, but their progress was frustratingly slow.

One man was forced to go out in the town. Silas Pow had been summoned by a distraught Mistress Findlay to visit her husband, Jamie. When he got to their cottage, he threw off his soaking cloak and demanded to know what the man wanted.

Jamie was sitting on a stool, crouched over like a man twice his age. He shook his head as he spoke. "I can't do it," he mumbled.

"What are you saying?" said Pow. "Can't do what?"

"The witch ... the trial ... I'm feared of facing her."

"You've got to," Pow told him. "You are an important witness. You want rid of her, don't you?"

"Aye, but ..."

"Then you have to play your part."

"I told you what she did," Jamie cried. "You don't need me."

Pow took a deep breath to control his growing anger. "All you have to do is repeat it to the court," he said. "You will be called in and when you've finished, you can leave."

"She'll see me, don't you understand? She'll know it's me. She'll get back at me. Do a spell."

"Don't be ridiculous."

"She's a witch. She can do anything."

"You will be protected," said Pow. "We will make sure that you are safe."

"Nobody can be protected against her evil."

Pow felt like grabbing Jamie and shaking him. "Damn it, man, you wanted the trial," he shouted. "You can't back out now."

There was a silence, but after a moment Jamie slowly shook his head. "I can't do it." There were tears on his cheeks.

Pow regarded him fiercely. "You must," he said. "I will see that you are brought to the trial." He called through to Mistress Findlay who was in the cottage's other room. "I charge you in the name of the law not to let your husband out of this house until he is sent for."

She nodded fearfully and handed him his sodden cloak.

He hurried back to the manse, looking forward to drying out in front of the kitchen fire. But when he got there he discovered it was not lit. The minister had always done that, but he was in the tolbooth jail.

It was two hours before the trial was due to start. He was anxious to get on with it, but reluctantly he had to wait. He did not want to be alone with his thoughts. Doubts he wished to avoid crowded his mind. Discovering Pheemie hiding in the stable had been a triumph, but afterwards he was forced to consider its implications. He had assumed without question that she had transformed herself into a cat and then a bird. Equally, that the minister was under the influence of the Devil. He saw now that it was almost certainly a delusion. For the first time in his life he questioned the so-called supernatural powers of witches. His experience in Pheemie's garden had shown him how fear could drive a person to imagine the impossible. And worse — as his confrontation with Jamie had shown. The man was being driven mad by what he thought he had seen.

He looked out of the back window. The stable was being battered by the storm and he watched as the wind wrenched some pantiles from the roof. Had she been there all the time?

He was a man split in two. One half of him hung on grimly to his conviction that witchcraft existed and that those who practised it should be destroyed. But the other half of him — newly discovered though it was — had raised doubts he never expected to have. A sense of guilt crept over him. It was as though his whole life was being questioned. It was unbearable — that he, of all people, should entertain such doubts. His crusade against these diabolical creatures had become his reason for living. He could not give in now. It would be humiliating and worse, he might even be accused of being a fraud. He must carry on and dismiss any doubts about his work. He would be resolute. There must be no chinks in his armour.

He had been brought to Fife to do a job and it was a matter of pride that he should accomplish his task. Also he was much in need of the fee promised to him by Sir Robert Abercrombie.

"Listen to me!" cried the minister. He thrust his arm through the bars of his cell and grabbed the Bailie's arm. "In the name of God, you must delay this trial."

The Bailie pulled himself free. "It's out of my hands."

"It's illegal. The laird had no right to set it up."

"The sheriff has approved the trial," said the Bailie. "He knows the law better than you minister."

The minister banged the bars. "He's just Sir Robert's toady — as you well know."

The Bailie shrugged. "That is the way things are. I'm just a fisherman. I can't change the world."

The minister dropped his voice. "Very well — there is something I must tell you. It is for your ears alone. I have appealed to the Lord Advocate to stop this trial, on the grounds that it is not properly constituted. I am convinced it will be stopped."

"And how is he going to do that?"

The minister hesitated and gave a heart felt sigh. "I'm not sure. But I have no doubt he will take action. That is why you must delay these proceedings."

"There's little I can do ..."

"You're a member of the commission who will judge Pheemie," the minister went on urgently. "It should be possible to stretch things out. She has told me how you have been sympathetic to her."

"Only because of a lack of evidence against her," said the Bailie. "Seemingly there is now evidence. As an honest man, I can but listen to it and make up my mind."

"And as an honest man it is your duty to prevent a miscarriage of justice, or you will have the death of an innocent woman on your conscience."

The Bailie regarded the distraught figure of the minister through the bars. "I will bear in mind what you've told me. I'll promise no more than that."

"Thank you."

"But I would tell you I consider witchcraft to be the curse of the age we live in," added the Bailie, leaving Andrew to wonder what, if anything, he had achieved.

The troopers threw themselves down onto the straw. Wet and exhausted, they were glad of temporary shelter in a byre near the town of Leven. The captain knew he had to give them some rest, before the remainder of their journey. His map showed him that the road, such as it was, ended in three miles. At the village of Kirkton of Largo they must cut off onto nothing better than coastal paths.

The boys were in a worse state than the men. Unused to horse-riding they were sure the torments of hell could not be worse than what they had endured. The captain looked down at them. He was a hard man, but he showed them a little sympathy. "We're over halfway there now. That should cheer you up," he said.

"I never want to see another horse," groaned Murdo.

The captain laughed. "And I never want to see another boat. How you can work on them every day is a mystery to me."

"We'd not be at sea on a day like today," said Alex.

Captain Nicol checked the documents in his haversack. Fortunately they were wrapped in oilskin and had so far escaped the wet. "Thank heavens for that," he said. "I'm thinking I'd look foolish if I'd let the ink run on a warrant from the Lord Advocate." He put the documents back and addressed the boys. "So, you have problems with a witch in your town?"

"Aye," said Murdo. "But she's not a witch."

"I was told there's to be a trial. Somebody must think she is."

"The laird."

"And you don't. What makes you so sure?"

"We know her," said Murdo. "She's just an old woman."

The captain took out his snuff box, but on opening it found it had been penetrated by the damp. He cursed and snapped the lid shut. "I've seen one or two witches burned," he said. "The crowds get unruly. They need us to keep order." He shook his head. "I can't say it is a duty I enjoy. Seeing somebody being burnt alive is never pleasant, even if it is what they deserve. The lucky ones are dead before the flames get them."

"What do you mean?" said Murdo.

"It depends on the executioner," said the captain with a shrug. "If he's a decent man he'll finish her off with his knife first."

"Stab her ...?"

"Yes," said the captain. "If he doesn't ... well, I can tell you, the screams are hard to bear."

The laird made sure the sheriff had his accustomed morning tot of whisky before they left the castle for the tolbooth. In fact Sir Robert had seen to it that it was larger than usual, and the sheriff was in good humour as they sat in the coach.

"I must confess your request came as a surprise, Sir Robert," said the sheriff, steadying himself as a gust of wind caught the coach. "We haven't had a witch trial for some time."

"The one we have before us today concerns a troublesome baggage and we will be well rid of her."

"So I understand."

"I'm quite sure we'll have it all cleared up within the day," said the laird. "The pricker from Edinburgh is a good man."

"Talking of Edinburgh, I take it you have received our accreditaion from the Privy Council?"

The laird drew a breath and for a moment glanced out at the swaying trees and unremitting rain. "This is a small local matter, sheriff, which we can easily dispose of. It is certainly not worth troubling higher authority."

"It's the law, Sir Robert."

"But so are we, in these parts. *We* administer justice here — not some faceless figures in the capital. Waiting for their authority could take months."

The sheriff did not reply immediately. He may have been old, but he was not stupid. Sir Robert wanted him to give the impression of legality to the trial. He nodded to himself — it was not the first time the laird had used him in such a manner. Granting such favours had been profitable to him in the past and he assumed this one would be the same. And he knew the laird could upset his comfortable life if he did not get his way.

"I hear what you are saying, Sir Robert," said the sheriff. "Can you be sure word of this will not get out?"

"Of course it won't," he said bluffly. "We are a small community in the middle of nowhere. Good heavens, highland lairds dispense justice without any interference."

"True enough." The sheriff regarded his companion for a moment. "You must have good reason to get rid of this woman?"

"I have indeed, sir," said the laird with feeling. However he had no intention of revealing his deep loathing of Pheemie. She had mocked his authority in the most outrageous manner and would be made to suffer for it. Nothing would stop him getting his revenge.

The sheriff did not question him further. He knew very well that the laird was a law unto himself, and as one of the aristocracy, used his privileged position for his own ends. "I agree that it is our duty to uphold the law in local matters. As you imply, we understand them best."

"Exactly so," said the laird. "I was sure of your co-operation."

"It is my pleasure, Sir Robert."

Old Pheemie sat on the straw in her cell remembering how she had met Murdo, her very first friend. She smiled. It was hard to believe a young lad would have time for an ugly old woman. But it had happened. She shook her head and looked across the cell at the minister. He was crouched in a corner and she thought he might be praying. They had said all that could be said to each other and lapsed into silence. In truth she was glad. He never seemed to stop talking. She supposed it was because he was a minister and he couldn't help it. She was much more used to silence — it was less trouble and less tiring.

An eye glinted in the straw. Pheemie remained still and eventually a rat appeared and looked at her. She stayed silent. If she'd said anything, she would have disturbed the minister and he would have frightened the rat away. She put her finger out and the rat sniffed it and then sat down beside her.

She wondered about the business of turning yourself into an animal. She couldn't think of anything more absurd. It was as daft as saying a person could will herself into becoming a table, or a chair. And yet the people who were about to put her on trial believed it. If she'd had a different life, would she have been like them? If her mother had not been a beggar and she had grown up handsome and not deformed. Would she have believed in witches and their diabolical powers?

Pheemie gently stroked the rat with her finger. It was a hard question to answer, but uneasily she realized the answer was probably yes. She would have wanted to be like everybody else and not be seen to be different. That was how people lived their lives. Even to the extent of believing the impossible.

Old though she was, she had been fortunate to meet Murdo and Andrew Robertson. Had she not, she would have died believing the whole world was against her. It was a comfort and would help her through the ordeal she was about to face. Silas Pow had horrified her when they came face to face at her arrest. His smile would have turned the milk sour. What hope had she against such a man?

There was a noise at the top of the stair leading down to the cell. The rat ran away into hiding and Pheemie wished she could do the same. The minister stirred and they both watched the town officer come down the stairs. He unlocked the cell door and spoke to Pheemie.

"They're ready to begin," he said. "You're to come with me."

Captain Nicol and his troopers stood looking at the remains of the wooden bridge they should have crossed. The weight of the water rushing down the swollen burn had smashed the structure to pieces.

"Damn and blast!" he swore.

The two boys didn't dare speak for fear of his anger. But they knew it was an awful blow. They had finally reached the bridge after a fearful slog over a poor water sodden track. One trooper had lost control of his horse and it had fallen and broken its leg. The animal had had to be shot, casting even more gloom over the troop.

"Get down and hold this," the captain ordered the boys, tossing a groundsheet to them. He squatted with his back against a stone dyke and they were meant to hold the groundsheet over him.

"Keep it steady, damn you," he shouted.

It was like holding a sail at sea, but they did their best to stop it flapping and blowing away. The farmer whose byre they had used, had sketched a rough plan of the route they should take. The captain studied it.

"There's another bridge further up stream," said the officer. "We must go up to that."

"How far is it?" Murdo risked saying.

"How the hell should I know?" snapped the captain.

12

The trial took place in the upper chamber of the tolbooth, the room normally used for town council meetings. It had been re-arranged to allow the public to watch the proceedings and the benches were crowded. Wet woollen clothes gave off an unpleasant stink as they slowly dried in the warmth.

The sheriff wrinkled his nose as he took his place at the table prepared for the commissioners. He was joined by the laird and the Bailie. Silas Pow seated himself at the side of the table.

"We are here to determine the innocence or guilt of the woman known as Old Pheemie, on a charge of witchcraft," said the sheriff.

"Everybody knows she's a witch," a voice shouted. Others called out their agreement.

The town officer banged his pike on the floor for order.

The sheriff did not reprimand them. "Now, the law says this. The accused must admit that she is, or was, in a Demonic Pact with the Devil, if she is to be convicted."

"Burn her!"

"That will do," said the sheriff sharply. "We will proceed in an orderly manner, or I will clear the court." He referred to a document in front of him. "We are empowered to employ all legal means to obtain a confession."

There was an audible reaction from the public benches and everyone looked at Silas Pow. They guessed why he was present at the trial and were anticipating what he would do to the witch to make her confess.

"Bring her in," the sheriff told the town officer.

Old Pheemie was led into the chamber and placed in front of the table.

"State your name, woman," said the sheriff.

"Euphemia McCleod," she told him.

"Are you not known as Old Pheemie?" asked the sheriff.

"Not by me."

The sheriff turned to the laird. "Sir Robert ...?"

"That's her. She's just being awkward."

"The court will call you Pheemie," the sheriff said. "It is said that you are friendly with the Devil. Is this true?"

"No."

"You have been seen talking to him."

"It's not true."

"It has been reported that on the night of 10th September 1672, you met the Devil in Den Woods," the sheriff told her.

Pheemie shook her head. "I couldn't have met him. I don't know what the Devil looks like."

"An owl," said the sheriff. "A *large* owl," he added, consulting his notes. "Well?"

"An owl? Who told you that — Glaiket Jock?"

"That's of no matter," snapped the sheriff. "You were seen consorting with the Devil in the form of an owl."

"It was just an owl."

The laird spoke up. "But you admit talking to it?"

"Aye, what's wrong with that?" said Pheemie.

"You are here to answer questions, not ask them," the sheriff told her. "The fact remains, that it is well known the Devil often appears to his servants in the form of an animal."

To their astonishment Pheemie laughed.

"Stop that at once," said the sheriff. "This is a serious matter."

"I have a blether with lots of different animals," Pheemie told him. "Are you saying they are all the Devil?"

"I told you — *you* do not ask questions."

The Bailie spoke to her. "Do you not admit it is a queer way to behave — talking to animals?"

"I've nobody else to speak to," she replied. "If we weren't here, none of you would give me the time of day."

"Guard your tongue, woman, or you will be held in contempt of court," said the sheriff sternly.

Pheemie sniffed. "I can't see that'll make any difference."

The sheriff consulted the laird and the Bailie, and then ordered that Jamie Findlay be brought in.

Much to the surprise of the public, there was a disturbance and it became clear Jamie did not want to enter the room.

Silas Pow went to help sit the man down. He spoke to the panel of commissioners. "Gentlemen, this poor wretch is still suffering from the evil influence of that woman. He was unfortunate enough to witness her transformation into a bird and it has grievously affected his sanity."

The sheriff regarded Jamie, who was being held in his chair. "Jamie Findlay, you are an important witness," he told him. "Do you understand why you are here?"

"Save me from her," Jamie cried.

"Sir, if it will help, I can repeat Findlay's testimony to me," said Pow.

"I would prefer that the man spoke for himself," said the sheriff. "Jamie, tell us what happened — what did she do to you?"

Jamie muttered incoherently and squirmed in his seat. The Bailie was shocked at the change in Jamie.

Of them all, he had little cause to feel sorry for him after their fight. But he seemed on the point of madness. The man who had been his friend was utterly broken.

"Maybe it would be better if Master Pow gave the evidence," suggested the laird.

The sheriff sighed. "Very well. Take Findlay away. Go on, Master Pow."

Before he could speak Pheemie interrupted. "I never become a bird. It was a ploy to stop him spying on me."

She was ordered to hold her tongue and Pow addressed the court. "As a good Christian man, Jamie Findlay was watching the on-goings at her hovel, in the hope of collecting evidence. Evidence of her black magic. And in so doing, he became its innocent victim. He saw this woman change into a black bird that chased him through the woods." He shook his head sadly. "You have seen the tragic consequences of the man's ordeal."

The Bailie questioned Pheemie. "What did you mean — when you said it was a ploy?"

"He'd put Murdo off his boat because the laddie knew me," she replied. "Such foolishness cost Murdo his job. And here he was, the same Jamie Findlay, spying on me. I made up my mind to frighten him off. And so we did. We tricked him into thinking I'd become my pet jackdaw."

Several people chuckled on the public benches.

"Silence!" ordered the sheriff. "Who was this boy? Why is he not in court?"

"He is a ruffian who was indeed involved with her," said Pow. "The fact that he ran away when he heard there was to be a trial speaks for itself."

"He's a good lad," protested Pheemie.

"Woman, you will speak only when spoken to," the sheriff told her. "I will not have these interruptions."

"Sir, I submit that Jamie Findlay's evidence gives us proof of her guilt," said Pow.

"I agree," said the laird. "I interviewed him soon after the event and can confirm he was terrified."

"Thank you, Sir Robert," said the sheriff. "Such corroboration is of great value." He turned to the Bailie, expecting his agreement.

"So it is," said the Bailie. "But it seems to me we are missing a vital witness — the boy. All we have at the moment is the word of a half-crazed man."

"That in itself is proof of her demonic powers," the laird retorted. "He was a fine upstanding man in the community before she got at him."

The sheriff glared at Pheemie. "You say it was trickery. And I say you are right — it was *diabolical* trickery, prompted by your master the Devil. What do you say to that?"

"It's not true," Pheemie replied. "I don't know how to do these things." She pointed at the laird. "He wanted me to change the wind, but he soon found out I couldn't."

"How dare you accuse me of complicity with witchcraft," blustered the laird.

"You mind how he took me to the castle, Bailie?"

The laird answered angrily. "You were taken to the castle because it was my duty to verify the belief that you had prevented the fishermen from putting out."

"You were feared for your own boat," said Pheemie.

"Be quiet, woman," snapped the sheriff. "If you continue these interruptions I'll have you put in irons."

"Sir, with respect, we are straying from the main issue," said Silas Pow.

"We are indeed," agreed the sheriff. "You have a further point, Master Pow?"

"Yes, sir. I would like to remind the court of the nature of witchcraft as it has been observed throughout the ages. Satan — the evil one — reveals himself here on earth through the medium of the creatures he has subverted. Namely, witches. Their every word and act is in his service. Even as we sit here, he is present in the shape of this woman, putting lies into her mouth as we strive to do our duty. In making a mockery of justice, she is serving his purpose. We would do well to remember that."

The sheriff nodded sagely. "A point well made, Master Pow." He addressed Pheemie. "Listen to me, woman. I am going to ask you a simple question. Are you, or have you ever been, in a Demonic Pact with the Devil?"

There was a silence and every person in the room looked at Pheemie. There were tears in her eyes and the Bailie was reminded of meeting her when she was looking for Murdo. Then, as now, she appeared no more than a worried old woman.

Pheemie shook her head.

"Speak, woman."

"No," she said.

The sheriff showed his annoyance. "I'll ask you once more. Were you doing the Devil's bidding?"

"I've told you, no," she cried. "Why can you not leave me alone?"

Silas Pow indicated that he would like a quiet word with the sheriff. While they were talking, John Reekie, the Bailie, told the town officer to give Pheemie a chair to sit on. The laird showed his disapproval, but John paid no attention. He realized that he believed her story about tricking Jamie Findlay, reasoning that Murdo would never have been involved in witchcraft. Like any lad of his age, he would have been too frightened. And he could appreciate her desire to punish the prying Jamie.

The sheriff addressed the court. "Since the defendant refuses to confess her guilt, we have no option but
to put her to the test. I had hoped this would not be
necessary, but there is no choice if justice is to be seen
to be done. Master Pow."

The pricker opened his wallet of needles and laid it
on the table. "All witches have the mark of Satan somewhere on their body," he said. "By pricking this mark,
it is possible to prove she is in league with the Devil. In
this particular case I have no doubt whatsoever where
I will find his mark. It is obvious for all to see. Take off
your shawl," he ordered Pheemie.

She undid her shawl and let it fall to the floor, leaving her humped back clearly visible. The chamber was
hushed. Pow spoke to the town officer. "Hold her," he
said. The man stood in front of Pheemie and held her
arms. Pow tore her garment until the hump was uncov-
ered. There were gasps from those watching.

He selected a needle and thrust it into a space at
the top of Pheemie's deformed spinal column. She did
not cry out, or make any reaction. Pow stepped back.
"Would you care to bear witness, sir?" he asked the
sheriff. "As you will see, there is no blood."

The spectators held their breath as the sheriff examined the old woman and nodded.

"Surely it requires more time," said the Bailie.

Pow leered at him. "I assure you, Bailie, more time
will not make a scrap of difference."

"It's a trick."

"No, sir," said Pow. "Like it or not, we have the Devil
by the tail here." To prove his point he inserted another
needle into Pheemie's hump. "See — no blood, no pain."

Pheemie suddenly spoke, surprising those clustered
round her. "I could have told you I wouldn't feel nothing. My hump's never had no feeling."

"What do you say to that, Master Pow?" asked the sheriff.

"A typical response, sir. Do not forget, she is being told what to say."

John Reekie picked up one of the needles off the table and examined it. "There is no trick, Bailie, I assure you," Pow told him.

John gritted his teeth and suddenly pricked Pheemie's arm with the needle. She cried out in pain and blood trickled down her arm. "You might ask him to explain that, sheriff," said John.

"This is outrageous," the laird protested.

"I suggest we return to our chairs," said the sheriff.

"Don't you see?" said Pow. "It's *his* work — the Devil. Making her bleed like that."

"Thank you, Master Pow, remove the needles, we have concluded the test."

"And proved nothing," said the Bailie.

"We will consider your opinion in due course, Bailie," the sheriff went on. "For the moment it is my duty to repeat my question to the defendant. Pheemie, do you have a pact with the Devil?"

Blood oozed through her fingers as she held her hand over the arm that had been pricked.

"No."

"Believe you me, I will remember this, Bailie, and it will not be to your liking," said the laird.

John Reekie faced him and spoke with a steady voice. "I do not think we can accept the pricking as firm evidence of her guilt."

The sheriff had declared a short adjournment and the four men were gathered in a side room.

Silas Pow spoke to the sheriff. "With respect, sir, you gentlemen have little or no experience of pricking. It has been found to be tried and true throughout Scotland. The fact that she bled from the arm is no surprise. Of course she would! We are looking for the Devil's Mark, remember — and she did not bleed or feel pain from that. *That* is the crucial factor. There is our evidence."

"I agree," said the laird.

"You would send a woman to her death on the strength of that?" demanded the Bailie.

"Damn it man, we know she's a witch. Ask him." The laird pointed at Pow. "He's seen more witches than you've had plates of porridge."

Pow nodded respectfully. "She shows all the signs. And I repeat, finding the Devil's Mark is conclusive."

"Exactly," echoed the laird. The sheriff looked round the group. "So, we find her guilty?" he asked.

"You are forgetting what you yourself stated in the court," said the Bailie. "She must *confess* — that is the law."

"Yes, yes of course," the sheriff blustered. "It is the legal requirement. We cannot be seen to neglect that. The question is, where do we go from here? Master Pow?"

"We must swim her."

"Ah, yes," said the sheriff, not fully comprehending what was entailed. "Perhaps you could detail the procedure for us."

"It is a simple test designed to overcome a defendant's reluctance to confess. Nature itself provides the answer, without the woman herself having to utter a word."

"How does that happen?" asked the Bailie.

"She is taken to a loch, bound hand and foot, and thrown into the water. If she sinks, she is deemed guilty of consorting with the Devil. If she floats, she is innocent."

The men were silent for a moment. All that could be heard was the wind and rain rattling the windowpanes.

"You mean we would all have to go to the town loch to watch this?" said the sheriff, glancing at the window.

"Yes sir," said Pow. "But I can assure you, it is more than likely that it will reveal her guilt. And her punishment will quickly follow thereafter."

"You mean she will drown?" asked the Bailie.

Pow shrugged his shoulders in reply.

"Then it must be done," said the laird. "It is the correct legal procedure. We need have no qualms about carrying it out."

"That may be so, Sir Robert," said the sherrif "But the weather is appalling."

"So be it, sir. We cannot be seen to shirk our duty because it is raining."

"You are right, I'm afraid," said the sheriff reluctantly. "Bailie, I trust you will arrange transport and a guard for the prisoner?"

When the public heard what was going to happen there was a mixed response. Few relished the thought of the mile long tramp to the town loch in such foul weather. On the other hand, it was a spectacle no one had expected and something not to be missed. Hats were pulled down firmly and plaids wrapped round tightly against the elements.

After he had ordered the town officer to find a suitable cart for Pheemie, the Bailie mingled with the excited crowd. The minister's words came back to him, urging him to delay the trial. Now he was certain he had no other course of action. The trial was fixed — he would be outvoted whatever he said. Conscious of his inability to influence the result, he resolved to do what he could to cause a delay.

Elbowing his way through the throng he found the person he was looking for. Glaiket Jock was sheltering in a doorway, excited by the sight of so many people. John attempted to calm the lad. It was important that Jock fully understood what he was being asked to do. Seeing the money in the Bailie's hand did the trick.

Pheemie was bundled into a cart and the town officer recruited the laird's men, Tam and Rab, as extra guards.

He threw some rope into the cart. "I'll lead the horse," he told them. "You can get in beside her."

"Not me," said Tam.

"Me neither," added Rab. "We'll walk along side."

"She'll not harm you," said the officer.

"You're forgetting, I seen what she can do," said Tam.

"I doubt even she can do any witchcraft in this weather."

"Don't you believe it," said Tam. "This storm's her doing, as sure as fate."

"Get moving!" The sheriff shouted at them from the laird's coach. "The sooner we get there, the better. Where's the Bailie?"

"Here, sir." John Reekie hurried to the coach and got in beside Silas Pow, opposite the other two.

A straggling procession made its way out of town. The crash of thunder and lightning frightened more than the horses. Many of the townsfolk saw it as the Devil fighting for his own. It was a battle of good against evil.

Pheemie held onto the sides of the cart. When it was not jumping up and down, it swayed from side to side on the rough track. She understood the ordeal they were going to make her suffer and that it would end with her being drowned. Death didn't frighten her, but the

thought of the suffering beforehand made her shiver
with fear. She was an innocent woman, but it seemed
there was nothing on God's earth to help her prove it.
The minister's effort to stop the trial had failed. No
doubt the Lord Advocate was too busy with important
affairs of state to bother about a wee local trial.

She would die before she saw Murdo again. He had
changed her life. It was as though his friendship had
put blood back in her veins and given her a purpose for
living. Who would have believed it, at her age?

The cart lurched suddenly, throwing Pheemie off
her balance and she fell onto the floor of the cart. The
horse had stopped, but it was whinnying and tugging
to break free. The town officer was hanging on to the
bridle with both hands, trying to control the animal.
Pheemie stayed sitting on the wet straw. She could not
see over the sides, but she could hear a great commotion going on. People were shouting. And even through
the noise of the wind and rain, she could recognize
what they were crying out.

"Cold iron! Cold iron!"

She laughed — something she'd never expected to
do in her present misery. They'd have a hard search to
find iron out on the track to the loch. A pig, it had to
be. She pulled herself up and saw people running in all
directions. And there *was* a pig. A beautiful pig, pink
and white in colour, the mud on its body washed clean
by the rain. The animal was confused. It trotted this
way and that, unsure of where to go in the unfamiliar
surroundings.

People rushed to the laird's coach to touch its iron-
work.

"What on earth is going on?" demanded the sheriff,
totally bemused at the crowd suddenly surrounding the
coach.

"They are touching iron, sir," said the Bailie. "They have seen a pig."

"A pig ...?"

The laird swore. "The stupid fools think it brings bad luck," he told the sheriff.

"Folk are running all over the place," said the sheriff. "It's ridiculous, being held up like this."

"Bailie, you are the magistrate," said the laird. "It is your responsibility to restore order."

"I very much doubt I can do that, Sir Robert. None of the fisherfolk will go near that animal."

"Then you and the officer must take charge and remove it," the laird said.

John Reekie shook his head. "It is not possible, Sir Robert. I am a fisherman and the officer comes from a fisher family. We cannot risk it. That creature is a manifestation of evil."

"That's nonsense," shouted the laird.

"Not to a fisherman. The Devil inhabits that animal and his evil seeps out of its trotters. Were we not to avoid it, there would not be another fish pulled from the sea."

"What are we to do?" cried the sheriff. "We must get the witch to the loch."

"Surely the pig will run away of its own accord," said Silas Pow. "It must be frightened." He got out of the coach. "I'll see where it is now."

The horse had been freed from the shafts of Pheemie's cart and the back end was resting on the ground. Pheemie herself was sheltering from the rain under the cart. She was talking to the pig, which was standing beside her.

Pow knew very little about farm animals, but he was confident he could scare the pig away. Pheemie and the pig both looked at him as he approached through the rain. He stopped and waved his arms. The pig didn't move. He waved and shouted, with the same result. Then he ran at the pig. This time it did move, but stopped only a few yards away. Pow ran at it again and the pig trotted back to where it had been before. Pow stamped his sodden boot on the muddy track. Clearly he must keep on chasing it if he was going to get it away. He took a deep breath and ran at the beast and kept after it. Puffing and blowing, he followed the pig for some time, until he realized they were going round in a circle.

With the little breath he had left, he cursed and returned to the coach. The pig went back to Pheemie.

"I've done what I can," he said, flopping back in his seat.

"With what result?" demanded the laird.

"The pig's still there."

The four men sat in disgruntled silence. The Bailie had no way of knowing if the delay would be long enough. Perhaps he should have questioned the minister further? His hope was that they would be held up until nightfall and the swimming would be put off to the following day.

Slowly people gathered in a wide circle around Pheemie and the pig. They were ready to dash off at a moments notice, but nevertheless fascinated to see what would happen. The Bailie joined them, willing time to pass and the grey sky to turn black.

"It's a grand pig, Bailie," said Glaiket Jock, appearing beside him.

John Reekie hushed him and praised him in a lowered voice. "Aye, Jock. You did well."

"What's wrong with pigs, Bailie?" the lad asked him.

It was a difficult question for John to answer. He'd grown up with the superstition and accepted it like every other fisherman. Even though the pig was serving his purpose at the moment, he still felt revulsion towards it. "Some animals are bad, Jock." he said.

Jock nodded wisely. "Like the witch."

"It's a wee bit the same," said John, trying to express himself simply. "It's what folk think."

"Are they going to burn Old Pheemie?"

"I don't know."

"They'll never get a fire going today," said Jock.

Silas Pow came squelching up to the Bailie. "We'll soon be on our way," he told him. "I've taken action — something you were less than keen to do, I notice."

John regarded him with loathing. "And what do you mean by that?"

"I think that's obvious, Bailie."

"You can take that remark back."

"No, sir," said Pow. "You forget, my trade is unmasking liars. I know one when I see one."

John Reekie's impulse was to punch the man, but before he made a move there was the sound of a musket shot. An excited cheer went up from the crowd. The pig had been killed and lay on the ground beside Pheemie. The town officer lowered his musket. Pow had sent him back to the tolbooth to get it.

The Bailie watched Pheemie being prodded back into the cart. Silas Pow spoke to him. "You see, Bailie, there *was* something that could be done — even by a superstitious fisherman — *if he had been so minded ..."*

13

When the troopers arrived at the town it was deserted. Their horses' hooves clattered down the cobbled streets as they searched for any sign of life. When they reached the tolbooth Captain Nicol jumped off his horse and ran into the building. The trial chamber was empty and he went down the stairs to the cell where he found the minister banging on the bars. He hurriedly told the captain about the swimming. "Go quickly," he urged. "Though I fear you will be too late."

The troopers and the boys were just beginning to enjoy the shelter of the tolbooth when the captain ordered them out again. Grumbling, they re-mounted their sodden horses and rode into the storm.

"I will pray for you," the minister called after them.

The sheriff and the laird watched the proceedings from the shelter of their coach.

Under the supervision of Silas Pow, Pheemie's arms and legs were bound with rope. He spoke to her. "This is your last chance to confess. Are you, or have you ever been, in a Demonic Pact with the Devil?"

She did not reply. A final spark of obstinacy shone in her eye and still she would not bow to her tormentor.

"Put her in the boat," Pow ordered.

Rab and Tam dumped Pheemie on board as if she was a sack of oats. They quickly backed away and Pow prepared to board. It was his task to toss her into the water and decide whether she sank or floated.

The crowd of townsfolk appeared to relish Pheemie's harsh treatment, no doubt believing it was what she deserved. However, the sight of the old woman trussed like an animal made John Reekie feel sick. Like everybody else, he was used to death and cruelty. It was the way of the world. But this was too much, and Pow's sadistic pleasure in what he was doing was the final straw.

He ran to the boat, shoved Pow out of the way and pushed the boat out onto the loch. With the wind behind it, the boat was soon out of reach from the shore.

A loud cry of protest went up from the crowd.

"You damned fool!" Pow screamed. "Get it back in," he shouted at the town officer.

"Leave it," ordered the Bailie.

"Bring it back," cried Pow.

"No." The Bailie stood as though on guard.

Pow ran to the laird's coach. "The man's gone mad. It would be over and done with by now, if he hadn't interfered."

The two men got out of the coach and squelched across the soggy grass to confront the Bailie.

"This is unforgivable," the sheriff shouted at him. "You are interfering in the due process of the law."

"You men — get that boat back in," the laird commanded. But Rab and Tam pretended not to hear and melted into the crowd. The laird was furious. "Somebody, anybody, I'll pay you well to bring that boat back." He swung round and faced Pow. "You — it's your responsibility. You bundled your job. Get it back."

"I can't swim, Sir Robert ..."

The bedraggled crowd grew angry and the laird and the sheriff found themselves having to pacify the cheated townsfolk. The situation was fast getting out of hand.

The feeling of calm that overcame Pheemie surprised her. The pain from her bound limbs had disappeared, as though her old body had finally grown tired of suffering. Lying as she was, she could only look upwards at the racing grey clouds. The rain falling on her face did not trouble her in the slightest. It was fresh and clean, and a relief from the men who were tormenting her. It did not occur to her to wonder what had happened. Her only thoughts, such as they were, were to be ready for death. If she wasn't dead already — and she didn't think she was — she was happy to go now.

If Pheemie had been able, she would have heard a distinct change in the noise from the bank of the loch. Galloping horses, men shouting, cries of fear from the crowd, would have told her that she had been saved. As it was, the first thing she noticed was that her gently floating boat suddenly began to rock from side to side. Two pairs of hands had grabbed the sides and Murdo and Alex hauled themselves up out of the water. Alex took the oars, while Murdo undid the ropes that bound Pheemie.

On the lochside the captain lost no time in apprehending the laird and the sheriff for staging an illegal trial. And Silas Pow was arrested for practising as a pricker without a warrant from the Lords of Council. The three of them were herded into the cart that had brought Pheemie to the loch.

Sir Robert was wild with rage. "Damn it sir, we are gentlemen. You have no right to treat us like this. There is no reason why we shouldn't ride in my coach."

"Yes there is," Captain Nicol retorted. "I have commandeered it to be used in the King's service."

When the boat reached the bank a trooper stooped down and gently lifted up Pheemie in his arms.

"Is she all right?" the Bailie asked.

"Aye — she's fine," said the man.

John Reekie sighed. "Thank God," he said.

The captain had Pheemie and the two boys put into the laird's coach, where they were wrapped in travelling blankets. Before he shut the door, the captain spoke to the boys. "If you were troopers, I would have you punished for irresponsible behaviour. I gave you no order to jump into the loch. What you did was a serious breach of discipline."

"But we got Old Pheemie," said Murdo.

Captain Nicol nodded. "Aye, so you did," he said with a grunt. "You are brave lads — but undisciplined. Make sure you keep yourselves warm," he added, slamming the door.

Murdo and Alex looked at each other and laughed. The contrast between their terrible journey and the luxury of the coach was unbelievable. They had never known that blankets could be so soft and upholstered leather seats so comfortable. Pheemie was seated opposite them, her eyes closed and her breath coming in short gasps. How she had survived was a wonder to them and they prayed the ordeal had not been too much for her.

To their amusement, they realized that the three of them were steaming as they began to dry out. The coach windows were steamed up and Murdo wiped one of them clear. They were heading back to the town, together with the remnants of the crowd. Murdo noticed a figure tramping along in the opposite direction to everybody else. As the coach drew level with him, Murdo realized it was the minister. He opened the window and shouted for the coachman to stop.

Soaking wet as he was, the minister's look of astonishment was like a ray of sunshine when he heard that Pheemie had been saved. Captain Nicol had released him from the cell, but he had been left to make his own way to the loch.

"Thank God," he cried.

"*And* these two lads," said a small voice from inside the coach. "Get in minister, out of the rain."

They found a blanket for him and he settled down beside Pheemie. "How are you feeling?" he asked her.

"Queer," she said. "I thought I'd left this world forever — but here I am, back in it."

"It's a miracle."

Pheemie thought for a moment. "You could be right," she said. "If yon pig had not turned up, I wouldn't be here now."

The minister and the boys knew nothing about the Bailie's efforts to delay the trial and guessed that Pheemie's old mind was imagining things. But they asked no more questions. They were exhausted and in the warmth of the coach they soon fell asleep.

Pheemie stayed awake for just a little longer. It was good to know she was still alive, she thought.

As Pheemie's mother used to tell her, fine weather usually follows foul. And so it was. The morning after the trial dawned clear and bright, the rising sun promising to bless the village with a fine day.

The fishermen were up and about early. There was hard work to be done. Their boats were up high on the beach because of the storm and had to be hauled back and made ready.

The captain also had his troopers up early, grooming and feeding their horses. The two horses the boys had used were also made ready for the return journey to Edinburgh. They would be used for the prisoners. The captain smiled with satisfaction at the thought of leading them up the High Street to the jail.

"I see you're making an early start, Captain," said the Bailie, arriving at the tolbooth.

"Aye, as soon as the men have had a bite to eat we'll be on our way."

The Bailie shook his head. "I never thought I'd live to see the laird arrested like a common criminal."

"According to the warrant he's got a lot to answer for."

"That's true enough," agreed John Reekie. "We all know there are rogues amongst the gentry, but in my experience they are rarely brought to justice."

"You have your minister to thank for that," said the captain. "Aye, and the lads. They did a good job."

"I must confess, I didn't think highly of the minister," said the Bailie. "The folk hereabouts called him a sweetie wife."

"Then they'll need to change their tune. It took a brave man to do what he did."

The Bailie glanced at the freshly groomed horses with an admiring eye. Only the best of animals were good enough for the King's Guard. "There's just one thing puzzles me. Why is the sheriff not being taken to Edinburgh?"

"He is not named on the warrant. I have no authority to apprehend him. Howsoever, he has been sent back to Cupar, knowing that I shall report on his conduct. I doubt it will not be long before Fife has a new sheriff."

John Reekie could not resist the temptation to go into the tolbooth and see the prisoners. Though in truth he found it strange to think of them like that. They were in the same cell in which he'd locked up Pheemie.

"You Judas!" Silas Pow shouted at him. "You will suffer the torments of hell for this."

"Be quiet," snapped the laird. He looked through the bars with disdain at the Bailie. Even in the grim surroundings of the cell he retained the usual haughty air he adopted with underlings. His arrogance did not appear to be dented by what had happened. It was a kind of aristocratic confidence that John Reekie could only wonder at.

"I've little to say to you, *Bailie.*" Sir Robert sneered as he said the word. "You will rue the day you decided to cross me. You will learn that questioning your superiors is a dangerous folly. I have friends in high places who will make sure you do not go unpunished. You will not be the first local magistrate to suffer for having ideas above his station."

"Talking of suffering, Sir Robert, you might consider what lies in store for you. The charges listed in the captain's warrant make interesting reading. Holding an illegal trial that could have ended in the murder of an old woman. Smuggling and authorizing the attempted murder of two innocent boys. I wonder what your high born friends will make of that?"

The captain came down the stairs to get the prisoners. Before he had time to speak, Silas Pow pushed the laird aside and was crying out to the officer.

"You are in error sir. I came here in good faith. I did not know the trial was illegal. Had I known, I would not have offered my services. I have an honourable reputation in these matters. This man tricked me. He wanted to use my expertise for his own nefarious ends."

The laird grabbed Pow by the scruff on the neck and shoved him across the cell.

"You see! You see!" Pow screamed. "He knows he's guilty. He traded on my innocent goodwill."

"You are wasting your breath on me," said the captain. "The Lord Advocate is the man who wants to hear your story."

"So he shall."

"He'll want to know how you came to be practising without a warrant from the Lords of Council."

"I was unaware that I needed one for such a trivial matter," Pow blustered.

"Don't play the daft laddie with me, sir," the captain told him sharply. "You've been in your unholy trade for years. You knew fine."

The laird spoke up. "For God's sake, get me out of here. This man will drive me mad — and he stinks."

A quiet, but curious crowd gathered outside the tolbooth to watch the troopers depart. The laird and Silas Pow were mounted, each of their horses led by one of the soldiers on a long rein.

Murdo and Alex were in the crowd. They were also silent. The enormity of what they had helped to bring about was suddenly made clear by the astonishing spectacle. None other than the laird was being taken away to face trial. For his life, the captain had said. The man who had held the power of life and death over the fishing community was now to be judged himself.

Nobody spoke. The troopers and their officer were grim faced and the people in the crowd seemed to be holding their breath. Hooves on cobbles were the only sounds to be heard and soon enough they had faded away.

"And how are you feeling today?" the Bailie asked the boys. "Not caught a cold from your dip in the loch?"

Murdo and Alex looked at each other and shrugged. They were still affected by what they had just been watching.

John Reekie nodded his understanding. "It occurred to me that you might be looking for a job?"

"Aye!" They both found their tongues together.

"Good. You can join my crew. Help get the boat down and then get to work on the nets."

"Mr Reekie," said Murdo, as they were setting off. "What's going to happen to Old Pheemie?"

"She's going to stay at the manse with the minister, as his housekeeper," he told him. "Though who will be helping who remains to be seen," the Bailie added with a smile. "They've already decided to keep some hens in the old stable."

On his way to the harbour the Bailie noticed Jamie Findlay sitting on a stool outside his cottage. He slowed his step, and then halted. Jamie was watching the boats being prepared. John Reekie wondered what he was thinking. His own thoughts were confused. In spite of the beating Jamie had given him, he felt sorry for his old friend. He had been cruelly punished — far worse than any revenge that John might have devised. He went up to Jamie and stood beside him.

They watched the activity on the harbour in silence. Then John spoke. "The laird used you, Jamie. Like he used the rest of us, for his own ends."

"She's a witch."

"No. She tricked you."

"I know what I saw," said Jamie.

"I don't doubt it," John agreed. "But you believed what you wanted to believe. We're all guilty of that."

Jamie shook his head and then nodded towards the sea. "Are you going out?"

"Aye."

"My crew think I'm off my head."

"Away with you," said John lightly.

"It's true." Jamie was like a man in pain. "It was the fear. It was unbearable, the fear I felt."

"There's only one way to put it right, Jamie," John said, stooping down beside him. "Show them they are wrong. And if there's one man who can do that, it's you. You're the best fisherman of us all. Get out there — shoot your nets. Put it all behind you."

Jamie gripped John's shoulders. "If only I could."

"You can. Come down with me. I'll back you up."

Tears filled Jamie's eyes. "You're a good man, John."

"Blethers," said the Bailie. "Come away now. We don't want to miss the tide."

DONALD LIGHTWOOD is a former drama adviser in Fife, with a wide experience of teaching and lecturing. He dramatized *The Baillie's Daughter* and *The Desperate Journey* for BBC Scotland. He is also the author of *Don't Forget to Remember, The Long Revenge,* and *The Wonder on the Forth.* He lives in St Andrews, Scotland.